FELIX ~~DIXON~~
AND THE
TRAITOR'S T

Collect all the 'Felix Dashwood' series:

☑ Felix Dashwood and the Traitor's Treasure

☐ Felix Dashwood and the Mutating Mansion

☐ Felix Dashwood and the Traitor's Revenge

Collect the 'Ghost Island' series:

☐ Ghost Post

☐ Doorway To Danger

About the Author

Luke Temple was born on Halloween, 1988. When he was 10, Luke didn't enjoy reading, he was terrible at spelling and he found writing hard work. Yet today he's an author! When not writing, Luke spends most of his time visiting schools and bringing his stories to life with the children he meets.

To find out more about Luke and his books, including fascinating facts, fun videos, downloads and hidden secrets, visit his website:

 # www.luketemple.co.uk

Felix Dashwood AND THE TRAITOR'S TREASURE

LUKE TEMPLE

Gull Rock Publications

Dedicated to Ben and Harriet,
who started me off on this adventure!

With thanks to Jessica Chiba, Catherine Coe, Gareth Collinson, Mike
and Barbara Temple, Kieran Burling and the Highfield Hall Jury

www.luketemple.co.uk

First published in Great Britain by Gull Rock Publications

ISBN: 978-0-9572952-2-3

Printed and bound by CPI Group (UK) Ltd, Croydon, CR0 4YY

A catalogue record of this book is available from the British Library

Thistlewick Island

The Note

I will not answer back. I will not answer back. I will not answer back.

Felix stopped writing and groaned. What she really wanted to write was 'I hate Mr Foxsworth. Mr Foxsworth is evil.'

It wasn't her fault that her homework book had got soaked in water on the way to school. How could she have known that her water bottle was going to leak all over it? She had told Mr Foxsworth as much and that's how she had ended up here, writing lines at the small table in the corner of his office on Friday lunchtime.

Everyone else was out on the playground. She could hear them, yelling and screaming and having fun. Even Mr Foxsworth had gone out, locking her in and saying that if she hadn't finished the whole page by the end of lunchtime she would get a full week of detentions.

I will not answer back.

Felix wasn't exactly the best behaved pupil at Stormy Cliff School – that was probably her best friend, Caspar – but she wasn't the worst either. Yet since Mr Foxsworth had become head teacher last month, he had given her six detentions and only one of them she'd really deserved. It wasn't fair!

Normally she would have hated writing lines and done it extra slowly, but she knew that Mr Foxsworth would carry out his threat if she didn't finish by the end of lunch. There was no way she wanted to be stuck in Mr Foxsworth's office every lunchtime now that Caspar was going to be leaving in a week's time. She needed to spend as much time with him as possible!

Felix and Caspar had grown up together on the small island of Thistlewick, an hour's boat ride from England. Although they were quite different – while Felix loved nothing more than diving into the choppy sea around Thistlewick, or chasing snakes through the rolling green grass, Caspar preferred to sit and read about adventures in books – Felix couldn't imagine life without him.

But now she was going to have to. Caspar's mum had lost her job recently and couldn't afford to pay the rent on their house any more. They would be moving to England next Friday and staying with Caspar's grandparents in Birmingham while his mum looked for a job. And there was nothing Felix could do about it.

I will not

The ink on the page stopped halfway through writing this sentence. Felix frowned at her pen and shook it. She put it back on the paper but still no ink came out, so she shook the pen harder. The next thing Felix knew, the piece of paper was covered in ink and all the sentences she had already written had disappeared under a mass of dark blue.

Felix thumped her hand down hard on the table. First her water bottle, and now her pen had leaked. Mr Foxsworth would never believe she hadn't done this on purpose. She used the piece of paper to mop up the rest of the ink from the table and carried this and the leaking pen to the bin, not caring that her hands were also covered in ink.

She went to her bag and searched around for another pen and piece of paper. All she found was a pencil, but she had no paper – her homework book was still wet. Felix looked around Mr Foxsworth's office and saw a notepad on his desk in the middle of the room. Just as she was about to rip the top sheet of paper from the notepad, the clock struck one o'clock.

Felix collapsed back into Mr Foxsworth's chair. It was only ten minutes until the end of lunch. She would never be able to write a whole page of lines in that time. She closed her eyes tightly. A full week of detentions! Now she would hardly get to see Caspar at all before he left for England.

She opened her eyes and stared blankly at the notepad in front of her.

If only Drift were here. He could talk his way out of anything. Just last week, he'd somehow managed to avoid getting into trouble even though he'd stolen the password for the computer in Thistlewick Island Hall, which Mayor Merryweather had decided only adults should be able to use. Drift had taken the mayor's notepad and rubbed a pencil over the next page down. He explained to Felix that if the mayor had written the password on the notepad, then the pressure of the writing would have transferred to the paper below it too. Sure enough, the pencil rubbing revealed the password: 'syzygy'.

She stared down at Mr Foxsworth's notepad and wondered what he had written on the last page that he had ripped out of it. Figuring she was already in plenty of trouble anyway, she started to rub her pencil across the notepad.

Nothing appeared as she shaded in the top half of the page but, as she kept going, two words appeared, in Mr Foxsworth's spidery handwriting: Treasure on. She kept rubbing and found the next word: Thistlewick.

Felix frowned. 'Treasure on Thistlewick?'

She rubbed right to the bottom of the page until it was completely covered in grey pencil marks. A few more words appeared: Tormenta, be quick!

'Treasure on Thistlewick, Tormenta, be quick!' said Felix. 'Mr Foxsworth is looking for treasure?'

She looked up as she heard the sound of a key turning in the door lock. She quickly ripped the piece of paper out of the notepad and thrust it into her pocket. The door swung open and a shadowy figure stood there.

Mr Foxsworth's shoulder-length greasy hair glowed

jet black and his eyebrows curled up evilly, like two devil horns. Felix looked into the blackness of his eyes as he glared at her.

'Get out of my chair,' he boomed.

'Sorry, sir.' Felix waited for the telling off she was about to get.

But Mr Foxsworth was examining the book he held in his hand, and seemed to have forgotten about Felix. He reached his chair.

'Leave,' he said. 'Now.'

Felix stared at him, surprised. 'There's ... there's still another five minutes of lunch left.'

'Leave,' he spat, baring his teeth like an angry dog.

Not quite believing her luck, Felix walked quickly out of the office before Mr Foxsworth realised she hadn't completed her lines.

The head teacher's office door slammed behind her. Had she really got away with avoiding a week of detentions? She rushed down the corridor to find Caspar, wishing for the millionth time he didn't have to leave.

That's when she remembered the notepaper in her pocket.

Her eyes widened. If there really was treasure on Thistlewick, then maybe Caspar wouldn't have to leave after all!

2
Fire!

'Hard to
starboard!' Mr
Skinner ordered the
helmsman. 'We're going
to hit 'em.'

The helmsman turned the wheel
of the *Doomsday* and the ship started leaning
right, away from the other ship, *Tormenta*.

'No!' yelled Captain Traiton, storming up to the
quarterdeck. 'You lily-livered fool. The closer the better.
I want to see the fear in their eyes. Hard to port!'

'They outnumber us two to one, Captain,' Skinner
cried. 'We don't stand a chance. Hard to starboard!'

The helmsman stood there, looking uncertainly
from Captain Traiton to Skinner, which infuriated the
pirate captain. He grabbed hold of the man and, with
an almighty swing, threw him over the wheel. Captain
Traiton watched the pathetic wretch land on the deck
below. He took hold of the wheel himself and steered
his ship closer to the *Tormenta*.

'Prepare for battle, men!' Captain Traiton yelled.

Below him, his crew yelled a fearless response.
'Yaaaaarrrrr!'

Captain Traiton ran his hands through his hair. His body buzzed with energy.

Since he was a boy he had led the life of a pirate. He had started as a powder monkey at the age of seven, watching his shipmates getting their legs and arms blown off around him. It had taught him to be fearless and only made him hungrier for the sea. By the age of thirty he was captain of his own ship, and kept a reputation as the fiercest pirate to roam the shores of Britain. Now fifty, he had captured many a ship in his time, but never one the size of the *Tormenta*. After planning his attack on this Spanish vessel for months, watching its every move in and out of the Spanish port of Santo Domingo in the Caribbean, he felt ready. Yes, the *Tormenta* was twice the size of the *Doomsday*, his current ship. Yes, it had double the number of cannons. But his men were a fine crew – they could fight fire and win.

Once the Tormenta *is mine, the oceans will truly belong to me!* he kept thinking.

'Prepare the cannon on the forecastle!' he called.

'Aye, Captain!'

Two men busied themselves with the task. A powder monkey fetched a cannonball, which was loaded into the cannon at the front of the ship. The cannon was angled and primed with powder.

'Ready to fire, Captain,' said Skinner, 'but I still don't think this is a good—'

'Fire!' yelled Captain Traiton.

The cannonball hit the *Tormenta*'s stern, splitting its railings in two with an almighty crack. The pirate captain smiled as he heard the cries coming from the other ship.

The *Doomsday*, being smaller and therefore faster than the *Tormenta*, picked up speed and was soon coming up next to it. But Captain Traiton saw that the *Tormenta* was ready – its portholes were open, its cannons primed.

He did not panic for an instant. 'Skinner, ready the men down on the gun deck!' he bellowed. 'Open the portholes on the port side. When we come alongside the *Tormenta* you are to fire across the length of the ship. Every man on the main deck is to take up position along the rails, or climb the rigging, aiming muskets at the enemy.'

There was a flurry of activity as the men prepared themselves. Captain Traiton skilfully guided the *Doomsday* in close. He looked across and saw the sailors on the other ship running about in panic. Their cannons might be prepared, but they were only a merchant ship, and their crew were unused to attack.

The two ships were barely twenty feet apart when the call came from the *Tormenta*. 'Fire!'

The *Doomsday* rocked under Captain Traiton as the cannonballs hit, sending splinters of wood flying into the waters below. The enemy were firing low on the *Doomsday*, aiming to sink it fast. He tightened his hold on the wheel.

The captain heard the boom of his own cannons

retaliating below. A sound that would strike fear into many hearts, but in his he only felt excitement.

He looked for the holes in the *Tormenta* where his cannonballs had hit. They were small – too small. This was indeed a mighty ship they were trying to capture! They'd need more than cannon fire to take it.

'Men, prepare your muskets. We'll take them out a man at a time if we have to!'

3

The Girls' Toilets

Felix looked across the playground and saw Drift swinging on the climbing frames, his school uniform as scruffy and covered in mud as Felix's. She walked over.

'What are you doing out here?' Drift asked, holding himself up on the monkey bars with one hand. 'I thought you had a detention?'

'I did. Mr Foxsworth let me out early.'

'He let you out early?!'

Felix laughed as Drift fell off the climbing frame in shock.

'Where's Caspar? I've got something to show you both.'

Drift nodded to his right. Felix's best friend sat against a wall, book in hand. He had been even quieter than normal since he'd found out he was leaving Thistlewick.

'Hey, Caspar, look at this.' She sat down next to him and pulled the piece of paper out of her pocket. 'It's from Mr Foxsworth's notepad.'

He put his book down and frowned at the note. 'Mr

Foxsworth is trying to find some treasure?'

'Isn't he rich enough already from being a teacher?' asked Drift.

'Don't know,' said Felix. 'But if there's treasure on the island, the last person I want to have it is Mr Foxworth!'

'Can you imagine how annoyed he'd be if we got it first?' said Drift.

Felix grinned. 'Yes! But we can't waste any time. The note says to be quick!'

Caspar narrowed his eyes at Felix. 'What do you mean?'

Felix shrugged. 'I think we should go and look for this treasure now. Mr Foxsworth has to be in school all afternoon. We could get a head start on him.'

'We also have to be in school all afternoon, Felix,' Caspar pointed out flatly.

The bell rang to signal the end of lunchtime. Everyone instantly stopped playing and froze. Mr Humdrum, Felix's class teacher, emerged from the main entrance and everyone started to line up in front of him. This wasn't because of Mr Humdrum – he was a grey-haired, deaf, old teacher that no one really listened to. These were Mr Foxsworth's orders.

Felix leant over to Drift. 'Let's hide.'

Drift nodded and they slipped behind a nearby bin.

'Come on, Caspar.'

Caspar looked from Felix to the single-file line of pupils and back again. He shook his head and joined the line. Mr Humdrum coughed and everyone started to trudge past him and inside like sluggish sheep.

'Mr Humdrum!' a voice shouted.

Felix peeked out from behind the bin, but she already knew who the voice belonged to. Mr Foxsworth's office window was open and he was staring out.

'Humdrum!' Mr Foxsworth roared again, when the old teacher failed to notice him.

'Yes?' Mr Humdrum croaked.

'You are missing two children. Behind the bin over there. Drift Castle and Felix Dashwood.'

Felix's heart sank. She was bound to get a week of detentions now.

Mr Humdrum squinted in their direction. 'Children? Come out from there, please.'

Felix and Drift slunk out from behind the bin and reluctantly went to stand behind Caspar in the line.

'Send those two to see me at the end of school,' Mr Foxsworth ordered. 'Now for heaven's sake go inside and get on with your lesson, Humdrum.'

The head teacher's window thumped shut and Felix shuffled along at the back of the line filing in through the main entrance. But as the rest of the class headed left, Felix nudged Drift and they both grabbed hold of Caspar by the arms.

'What are you—?' he began.

'In here,' said Felix, and they pulled him through a door on the right.

Caspar eyed up the room they were in – pink walls, sinks and toilet cubicles.

'Why have you dragged me into the girls' toilets?' A mixture of anger and panic spread over Caspar's face. 'We're going to be in so much trouble.'

He made for the door, but Drift blocked it. 'Don't be a wimp. Anyway, now we're out of Mr Foxsworth's sight, Mr Humdrum won't even notice we're missing. This is when he normally has his afternoon nap, remember?'

'Look, I don't just want us to find the treasure so we can stop Mr Foxsworth getting it,' said Felix. 'I want to find it for you, Caspar.'

'For me?'

'If there really is treasure out there somewhere, then we can use it to keep you on Thistlewick. We'll give it to your mum and you'll be able to afford to stay here.'

Caspar stopped panicking and bit his lip thoughtfully.

'Sounds like a plan to me,' said Drift. 'If it means we get to bunk off school.'

'But we don't even know for certain there is any treasure,' asked Caspar.

'There's got to be a reason for the note,' said Felix. 'And Mr Foxsworth's been acting strangely today – like when he let me off detention early. If there *is* treasure, we've got to get to it first! You know he'd only use it for himself.'

'He'd probably go on a cruise all summer or something,' Drift added.

'But if *we* find it, we can use it for something good,' said Felix.

There was a long silence. Caspar blinked and Felix couldn't read the emotion on his face.

'Please, Caspar, I really want you to stay on Thistlewick. I know you do too. This is our only chance.'

'Look, mate, if you're worried about getting into trouble, we won't,' Drift said confidently. 'And you're only meant to be on Thistlewick for another week anyway, so what's the worst that could happen?'

Another long pause followed.

Caspar sighed. 'I'm going to regret this, aren't I?'

Felix smiled and patted him on the back. 'Thank you.'

'Let's get out of here!' said Drift, grinning.

'But how?' asked Caspar. 'If we go through the main entrance, Mr Foxsworth will see us.'

Felix looked around and spotted the window above the sinks.

'We can climb out through the window!'

4

Charge!

The second round of cannon fire from the *Tormenta* hit the *Doomsday*. Captain Traiton let his ship roll sideways, giving his men by the railing a clear view of the *Tormenta*'s gun deck. The pirates fired their muskets, and the captain watched half of the enemy sailors fall to the deck.

A volley of musket and pistol shots hurtled back at the *Doomsday* from the main deck of the *Tormenta*. Captain Traiton ducked and several of his men flew to the ground, shrieking in agony.

The battle continued and shots rang back and forth between the two ships. Captain Traiton stood there, barely blinking, as bullets fired past him and ripped into the sails above. He was surprised – the merchant sailors of the *Tormenta* were showing more of a fighting spirit than he had anticipated.

He frowned as he saw them preparing another large gun on the *Tormenta*'s main deck. He unhooked his telescope from his belt to have a closer look.

Skinner ran up from below deck. 'Captain, that gun

they're loading, it fires chain shot. At this distance, we're doomed.'

'One more word of panic from you, Skinner, and I'll throw you overboard!'

Despite his words, Captain Traiton felt a small twinge of worry.

He had not planned to defend against chain shot, for it was uncommon on a merchant vessel. Not that there was much he could do. Chain shots were two heavy metal weights linked by a deadly chain, which could tear through almost anything. Captain Traiton had seen five men cut clean in half, one after the other, by a single chain shot. He'd just have to hope the merchant sailors had poor aim.

The rest of his men had noticed the gun too and were sharing fearful looks.

'Keep your cool, men!' shouted Captain Traiton. 'If any man shows fear, I will shoot him myself.'

He watched through his telescope as the gun was loaded.

'Take out the sailors operating that gun!' he yelled up to his men in the rigging.

But it was too late. The pirates in the rigging were being shot at with muskets.

'Fire!' the call sounded.

The shot tumbled towards the *Doomsday*, too fast for the eye to see, and broke the mainsail yardarm from the mast, tearing the huge canvas sail in two. Captain

Traiton looked at the damage, horrified.

Another shot came, hitting low down on the *Doomsday*'s mainmast and cutting straight through it. The captain had a sinking realisation that this was the end of the battle. The *Tormenta* had won. The mast swayed back and forth and pirates fled from under it.

A cheer rang up from the crew of the *Tormenta*. Captain Traiton turned away, but as a strange silence suddenly fell, his attention was drawn back to the ship. The sailors were staring at the *Doomsday*'s toppling mast. With a crash that sounded like all the thunder in the world combined, it fell over the side of the *Doomsday* and landed flat on the deck of the *Tormenta*, crushing several sailors under it.

What a stroke of luck! The mast had created a bridge between the two ships. Captain Traiton let out a roar of laughter.

'CHAAAARGE!' he called.

He jumped down from the quarterdeck, climbed up onto the thick mast and ran across it, followed by many of his crew, all jeering and yelling a bloodthirsty, 'YAAAAARRRRR!'

Yet more pirates threw rope attached to grappling hooks across and swung themselves over to the *Tormenta*.

The crew of the *Tormenta* barely had time to pull out their swords before Captain Traiton's men cut into them.

Captain Traiton pulled his huge sword out from his belt. No sword was longer or deadlier. He could see his enemy were inexperienced in hand-to-hand combat. If he was a man with a kinder soul, he might have let them surrender there and then. But he strode forward and hacked them down.

One man raised his cutlass above his head and charged at Captain Traiton. The pirate captain swiftly struck the sailor in the chest. Another tried to jump at him from the side. Captain Traiton caught this one by the neck and threw him overboard.

Captain Traiton did a quick calculation. It looked like the pirates now outnumbered the crew of the *Tormenta* that were left standing.

A small, balding sailor began to charge at him. The sailor went for his arm; the captain blocked with his sword and knocked the sailor to the deck with an elbow.

'Please, no! Show mercy!' the sailor pleaded in broken English, closing his eyes tightly as Captain Traiton raised his sword high above him, ready to stab down.

'Take me to your captain,' Captain Traiton growled, feeling triumphant.

'I ... I am de captain ... of *Tormenta*,' the puny sailor managed to get out.

'Then, sir, surrender your ship and I will kill no more of you.'

'I surrender! I surrender!'

With a shaking hand, the captain of the *Tormenta* handed Captain Traiton his sword.

The pirate captain raised it high and shouted, 'The *Tormenta* is mine!'

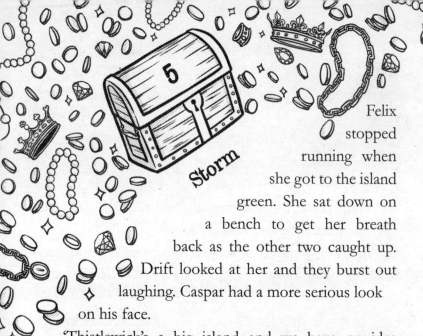

Storm

Felix stopped running when she got to the island green. She sat down on a bench to get her breath back as the other two caught up. Drift looked at her and they burst out laughing. Caspar had a more serious look on his face.

'Thistlewick's a big island and we have no idea where this treasure is, do we? It could be in one of the hundreds of caves, buried under one of the thousand trees in the forest...'

'Hidden under a sheep,' Drift chipped in with a smirk.

Caspar glared at him.

'You're worrying about it too much, Caspar. We haven't even started looking for clues yet,' said Felix.

'What clues are you expecting us to find?' he asked.

'You're the clever one, Caspar, why don't you figure that out?' said Drift.

Felix took out Mr Foxsworth's note again. 'Treasure on Thistlewick, Tormenta, be quick!'

'Do you know what "tormenta" means?' asked Drift.

'It's not an English word, is it?' said Felix.

'There's an English word, torment, which means to cause great pain or suffering,' Caspar explained, then added, 'Like you two are tormenting me now by forcing me to run away from school. But I've never heard of torment with an "a" on the end of it. It must be from a foreign language.'

'OK, so that's our first clue. We need to figure out what tormenta means,' said Felix.

'If we had stayed at school, we could have looked in the foreign language dictionaries in the classroom,' Caspar pointed out.

'We could go and look in your second home, Caspar,' said Drift. Felix gave him a quizzical look and he explained, 'The library.'

'No way. I'm not going to the library now. Mrs Turner knows me really well, and she'll know we're meant to be in school. We'd get into trouble.'

'So how else are we meant to find out what tormenta means?' asked Drift.

'We could use the computer in the island hall,' suggested Felix, 'now we've got the password.'

***

Standing on Drift's shoulders, Felix could just see through the window into the island hall.

'There's no one in there. Mayor Merryweather's

not at his desk – he must be out somewhere. Come on.'

She climbed down and they made their way round the crooked old building to the main entrance. Felix heaved the heavy oak door open.

'I'll stand outside to keep an eye out. If anyone comes near, I'll hoot like an owl,' said Drift.

'You can hoot like an owl?' asked Caspar doubtfully.

'Yep.'

'Prove it.'

Drift screwed his nose up. 'Baaaaa!'

'Come on, we don't have time for this,' said Felix. 'Let's get inside.'

Felix and Caspar left Drift guarding the door and walked into the island hall. The computer was in one corner, behind a giant flower arrangement. Felix soon turned it on and typed in the password: syzygy.

'Why is Drift such an idiot?' asked Caspar as Felix opened the internet browser.

'You're in a bad mood at the moment.'

'Are you surprised?'

'OK, then, grumpy, which language should we try first.'

Caspar shrugged. 'French, maybe.'

Felix found a website that translated French words into English and typed 'tormenta' in.

'No, it's not French.'

'German?'

Felix found a German website and tried it.

'Nope.'

'OK … Spanish?'

This time, when Felix typed the word and pressed enter, a translation pinged up on the screen.

'It's Spanish! Tormenta means "storm" in Spanish,' Felix read out. 'Come on, let's go and tell Drift.'

Outside, they found Drift doing handstands on the grass.

'I thought you were meant to be keeping an eye out,' said Caspar.

'I have been. No one's come anywhere near,' Drift replied as he stood back up again. 'So?'

'Tormenta is Spanish for storm,' said Felix.

'OK … so how does that help us?'

'Treasure on Thistlewick, the storm, be quick!' said Caspar. 'So the treasure has something to do with a storm on Thistlewick.'

'There are tons of storms around the island,' said Drift. 'My dad's always complaining about them – says they ruin his boats.' Drift's dad was a fisherman, and he also rented boats out to tourists.

At the mention of boats, Felix thought of something. 'Pirates!'

'What?' said Caspar.

'Well, that's who usually has treasure – and don't they bury it?'

'You think Mr Foxsworth is after pirates' treasure?' asked Caspar.

Felix nodded. 'It makes sense. Maybe it's from a pirate ship that sank in a storm.'

'But hundreds of ships have been wrecked in storms,' said Drift. 'Dad says being a fisherman is one of the most dangerous jobs on Thistlewick.'

'Anyway, if that's what Mr Foxsworth meant, then why would he write the Spanish word for storm and not the English?' asked Caspar.

'It could be a code,' said Felix.

'Give the note here a minute,' said Caspar.

Felix handed it to him. He ran a finger along the words, a deep frown of concentration on his face.

'Why does "Tormenta" have a capital letter?' he said slowly. 'It's not at the start of a sentence or anything.'

'What do you mean?' asked Felix.

'What has a capital letter when the word isn't at the beginning of a sentence?'

'Names,' Felix replied.

'So what if Tormenta is actually the name of something.'

'A ship,' suggested Drift.

'A pirate ship!' said Felix, excitement rising up inside her.

'It could be,' said Caspar.

'There's one way to find out. We need to go to the graveyard,' said Drift.

***

Felix stepped carefully around the gravestones spread out around the graveyard next to the island hall. Some were old and crumbling, covered in moss, others were better kept and Felix could still read the names carved into them.

They arrived at the monument that stood at the centre of the graveyard. It was the shape of a giant ship's sail and gleamed in the sunlight.

'Every ship that's ever been wrecked off Thistlewick is listed on this monument,' Drift explained.

'Wow, there are hundreds, aren't there?' said Felix, taking in the mass of old-fashioned, golden writing that covered the monument.

'They're in alphabetical order, too,' said Caspar, smiling.

'Only you could find that interesting,' Drift commented.

'It makes it really easy to find what we're looking for, though. Where does T begin?' asked Felix.

She stared closely at the monument. There were some unusual ship names: *Ballycumber* – 14 perished … *Giggleswick* – 87 perished … *Misty May* – 2 perished.

'The ship names only go up to M. *Tormenta* must be round the other side.'

She looked up and saw that Caspar was already standing on the other side of the giant sail.

'There's no *Tormenta* here,' he said.

Felix and Drift went round to join him.

'There's a ship called the *Toad* and another called *Trespasser*,' Drift noted.

'But no *Tormenta*,' said Felix. 'Maybe we're wrong. Tormenta must mean something else.'

She started to walk away from the monument.

'Hang on, maybe there's some reason why it's not on here. And there's something else we can try,' said Drift.

Felix stopped and looked at him, wondering what he meant.

'For it to work, though, we need three things,' he continued. 'An apple pie, a fresh bottle of milk and a perfectly rounded brown shell.'

6
Discovery

Having taken command of the *Tormenta*, Captain Traiton ordered the ship's former captain and all its crew to be tied to the railings of the *Doomsday*.

'Where is your honour, man?!' the former captain cried as he was tied up with rope on the *Doomsday*. 'You said no harm would come to us if I surrendered.'

Captain Traiton stared at the pathetic man. 'Gag him.'

Although the man tried to protest, a piece of cloth was easily forced into his mouth and secured with rope.

'Let's test out our new guns,' Captain Traiton said to Skinner. 'Tell the men to fire low down on the *Doomsday*.'

'Aye, Captain.'

A few minutes later, the *Tormenta*'s cannons fired. Captain Traiton beamed as he watched the wood of his former ship splinter into a thousand pieces and the men aboard it writhe and cry out in fear.

The *Doomsday* itself gave a dull groan. Water flooded into the holes. It was sinking fast.

Skinner ran up to Captain Traiton, on the quarterdeck of the *Tormenta*.

The pirate captain turned to him. 'And you doubted that we could capture this ship, Skinner. How foolish you are sometimes.'

'Captain, a discovery has been made below deck. You're going to want to see this for yourself.'

Captain Traiton noticed the glint in his second-in-command's eyes. He turned back to the *Doomsday*. The men on it were all holding their shaking hands up high, praying, as the stern end of the ship sunk into the water.

'This better be good, Skinner. You're ripping me away from all the fun up here. If I find it's for an unworthy cause, you will meet the same fate as those men on the *Doomsday*. Understood?'

'Aye, Captain. But I'm confident you'll want to see this.'

They climbed down to the gun deck, where the cannons were lined up – by far the finest cannons Captain Traiton had seen.

'Well done, men, an excellent aim,' he said to the pirates who had fired the final shots at the *Doomsday* as he passed them.

Their former ship had only had three levels, but the *Tormenta* had five. Skinner led the captain to the lowest one.

'Why are we in the hold?' Captain Traiton asked.

'Over there, Captain.' Skinner pointed to where a

group of pirates had gathered.

The captain pushed them all out of the way to see what they were staring at. What he saw took his breath away.

'I'll be damned. I knew the *Tormenta* was a fine ship to capture, but I did not know what cargo it held. No wonder they put up such a fight against us.'

He widened his eyes at the golden light of the treasure that filled a large, open chest. Gold, silver, rubies and gems of many magnificent colours. It was the stuff pirate stories were made of. He was rich!

'I claim this treasure as my own,' he announced, looking round his crew. 'And every man who sails under me shall receive his fair share of it!'

A deafening cheer rang out around Captain Traiton's new ship.

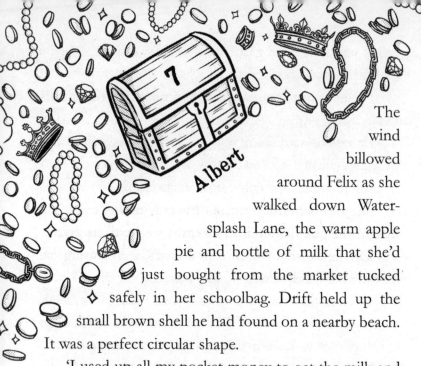

The wind billowed around Felix as she walked down Water-splash Lane, the warm apple pie and bottle of milk that she'd just bought from the market tucked safely in her schoolbag. Drift held up the small brown shell he had found on a nearby beach. It was a perfect circular shape.

'I used up all my pocket money to get the milk and pie, so they'd better be worth it,' said Felix. 'I get why you think we should talk to Albert. He's the oldest fisherman on Thistlewick, so if anyone knows if *Tormenta* is the name of a ship it'll be him. But why do we need these things?'

'I know Albert's tricks well. It's quite hard to get a story out him,' explained Drift. 'I'm hoping these things will help.'

'Bring back that fish, you pesky creature!' Felix heard a voice cry as they reached the harbour. 'You've taken what don't belong to you!'

As she walked down the steps behind the rickety old harbour hut, she saw Albert chasing a fat gull. The gull was squawking madly, to match Albert's shouts. In its beak it had a huge fish.

The harbour was only small, with barrels and nets lining its edges and a few traditional fishing boats tied to wooden planking. Albert was chasing the bird round and round in circles.

'Albert!' Drift called over to him.

The old fishermen turned towards them, and in an instant the gull fled up into a nearby tree with its prize.

'Oh, hello,' said Albert. 'That bird's been teasing me all morning and now it's stolen my best fish. What're you three doing out of school, 'specially in this weather? There's a storm brewing, you know. Have you come to see your dad, Drift? He's out fishing at the moment.'

'No, we wanted to talk to you, Albert,' replied Drift.

'We're doing a school project and we have to talk to an expert,' said Felix, thinking quickly. 'We're trying to find out about a ship. We think it's called *Tormenta*.'

The fisherman's bushy eyebrows knitted together. 'Your head teacher was here earlier asking about the same thing.'

Felix puffed out her cheeks. It was a good job they had escaped from school – it sounded like Mr Foxsworth really was trying to find the treasure quickly.

'Did you tell Mr Foxsworth anything?' asked Drift.

'No!' Albert replied sharply. 'He's a stranger on Thistlewick – only been here, what, a month? I don't go talking about such things to people I hardly know.'

'But do you know anything about *Tormenta*?' asked Felix.

'Oh, aye.'

Felix raised her eyebrows and shared a grin with Drift; even Caspar looked a bit excited. They were right – the *Tormenta* must be a ship. If they could get Albert to tell them what he knew, they would be one step ahead of Mr Foxsworth.

'Please can you tell us about it, Albert?' she asked in her nicest voice. 'You've known us for a long time.'

He stared at her suspiciously.

Drift stepped forwards. 'Look, Albert, we found this shell on our way here. We thought you might like it.'

Albert took the shell from Drift and his expression changed. His eyes lit up and his long, pointy beard twitched.

'Well, thank you, this is a beauty.'

Suddenly, a whole flock of gulls flew overhead and into the trees. Felix thought for a minute that they were all coming to fight the fat gull for the fish it had stolen from Albert, but the old fisherman knew better.

'Those birds are taking cover. They know the weather better than we do – the rain'll be here any second.'

Sure enough, thick, wet drops started to splatter down over the harbour. The wind blew the rain around and into their faces.

'I suggest we follow the birds' advice and take cover ourselves. Let's head into the hut,' said Albert.

***

Despite looking rickety and full of holes on the outside, the fishermen's hut was surprisingly snug and warm inside. It had a strong fishy smell, but Felix didn't mind – you couldn't grow up on Thistlewick without learning to love the smell of fish. Perched on a bench alongside Caspar and Drift, she listened to the rain rattling against the tin roof as the storm set in above them.

Albert was looking closely at the wall opposite them. Hung up on it was a large, half-finished mosaic of a mermaid, made entirely out of shells.

'How did you know that giving Albert that shell would get him so excited?' Felix whispered to Drift.

'That mosaic's his pride and joy. He's been working on it for about a year,' Drift replied. 'Watch…'

She did.

'Aha!' the fisherman cried triumphantly, pushing the brown shell into the mosaic and standing back to admire his work. The shell had become one of the mermaid's eyes.

'What do you think?' he asked.

'It's amazing, Albert,' said Caspar.

Felix looked at the clock on the wall. Time was going by fast. Soon it would be the end of school and Mr Foxsworth would be able to resume his hunt for the treasure. They had to hurry up.

'So can you tell us about *Tormenta*?' she asked.

Albert sat down in an ancient-looking armchair opposite them. 'Aye, I know of the *Tormenta*. Why, my great-great-great-great-grandfather himself, Capston Gailsborough, was the one who saw it when it came to Thistlewick.'

Up close, Felix thought Albert's wrinkles showed the very depths of the sea he sailed in.

'So *Tormenta* is a ship?' asked Caspar.

'It is.'

Felix waited for Albert to say more, but he didn't. Instead, he licked his lips thoughtfully.

'Feeling thirsty, Albert?' asked Drift, winking at Felix.

'Aye, I am.'

Felix picked up on Drift's signal and took the bottle of milk out of her bag. 'Would you like some milk, Albert? It's fresh.'

The fisherman's eyes lit up again and he held a cup out to Felix.

Once Felix had poured the milk, Albert sat back in his chair, took a sip and said, 'Let me tell you Capston's story…

'Capston was fond of stargazing and knew that the best place on Thistlewick for this was in the north of the island. After years of experience, he had discovered one spot atop a cliff that gave him the very best views of the night's sky. It was a spot he treasured and he had no desire to be disturbed when watching the stars, so he kept it as his secret. One evening in 1780 he set out in his boat and sailed round the coast to a northern cove. He climbed up onto his stargazing cliff and set up his telescope.

'Soon the weather turned bad and the worst storm Thistlewick had seen for years set in. Winds tore across the island and Capston felt the spray from the waves, even though he was right at the top of the cliff. There was no hope of him seeing the stars now. As the sky grew dark, Capston noticed a speck on the horizon. Looking through the telescope he recognised it as a boat – a grand ship – about half a mile away and lit by its own powerful lights. But what vessel would risk being out in such weather?

'As the ship got nearer, Capston was able to make out the ship's flag through his telescope. A skull and crossbones – a pirate flag if ever he saw one! Back in those days there was no way of getting in touch with the south of Thistlewick, and Capston couldn't risk rowing back in his boat with the sea like it was. All he could do was stand there and watch as the great ship came nearer to the shoreline. A thick mist had formed around it by now, and Capston saw this as a sign of the ship's evil. It drew closer to the island and through the mist he was just able to make out a name on her side.'

'*Tormenta*,' Felix gasped, her mouth wide open.

'Aye, the *Tormenta*!' Albert continued. 'The most feared ship in the whole of the Atlantic at that time. Its captain, who went by the name of Traiton, had captured

the ship from the Spanish two weeks before, and Capston had heard that half the Spanish navy were out looking for it. He realised where the ship was heading – straight for the very cove he was standing over. No captain in his right mind would send his ship so close to Thistlewick in such a storm, for the rocks around our island can be deadly, but a bloodthirsty pirate like Captain Traiton was probably not in his right mind. This only made Capston more terrified.

'Soon, he began to hear the chilling calls and shouts of the pirates. Convinced they were about to attack Thistlewick and fearing for his life, he ran quickly away, leaving his telescope and boat behind. Pirates had come to Thistlewick!'

Felix stared at Albert. He certainly knew how to tell a dramatic story.

'What happened next?' she asked. 'What did the pirates do?'

'There was no sign of Captain Traiton or his pirate crew on Thistlewick that night, or any after it. No one else saw the *Tormenta*. What happened to the ship is a mystery. I reckon Captain Traiton must have changed his mind and disappeared back into the storm, searching for another island to attack. When Capston spoke of his fears to his fellow islanders, some people believed him, but many did not and claimed he made it all up. After all, why would the scariest pirate ship around come to a place like Thistlewick Island? Capston's story has been passed down through my family, though, and I for one believe it.'

'Where was Capston when he saw the *Tormenta*?' asked Caspar. 'Where was his stargazing spot?'

'It was somewhere in the north, but alas, I cannot tell you more than that. As I said, it was Capston's secret spot, but I know that after that night he never returned there.'

Lots of thoughts fired through Felix's mind. Albert had confirmed what they thought about the *Tormenta* being a pirate ship, but Felix had a different idea about why it had come to Thistlewick – not to attack the island, like Capston had feared, but so that the pirates could bury their treasure.

If Captain Traiton had buried his treasure there, though, all they knew was that it was somewhere in the north of Thistlewick. Would they have to search the whole area?

Felix looked at the clock on the wall of the hut. It was half past three – the end of school. Mr Foxsworth was probably leaving right now, on his mission to find the treasure. They had to get to it before him, but with the whole of north Thistlewick to search, it could take a very long time.

She stood up and was about to thank Albert for his story when the old fisherman said, 'Capston was fond of writing poetry.'

'Sorry, Albert?' she said.

'Capston wrote a lot of poems. I think there was one he wrote about seeing the *Tormenta*.'

'Can we see that poem? It might help us with our school project,' said Felix, hoping there might be some clues in it.

'Well…' Albert rubbed his stomach.

'The pie,' Drift whispered.

'Oh!' Remembering it was in her backpack, Felix took it out. 'Would you like a slice of pie, Albert?'

'That is most kind of you,' he replied, taking the whole thing.

'You were talking about Capston's poems,' Drift reminded him.

'Ah, yes. My great-great-great-great-grandfather was a fine fisherman, but a dreadful poet. I have only read his poems once, and that was enough. Just before he died, he donated his whole book of poems to the Thistlewick Library. It is probably still there now.'

8

The Fortune-Teller

The *Tormenta* docked in the pirate port of Tortuga that night. After its battle with the *Doomsday*, it needed repairing. Captain Traiton also needed to find more crew, since it was a much larger ship.

Feeling generous, he gave his men permission to go ashore for the night and drink to celebrate their success.

When Captain Traiton stepped out onto the deck, he saw a line of sailors queuing outside the ship, seeking a job with him. Word must have got out that Captain Traiton had captured the finest of Spanish vessels, and he guessed they also knew of the *Tormenta*'s prize possession – its treasure. The line was so long that it snaked twice around the harbour. There were ragged-haired seadogs, men with muscles the size of tree trunks, others as tall as a house and many more in between. Captain Traiton would have the pick of the best of them.

He left Skinner with orders as to the number and type of sailors required and walked along the harbour wall to the town. A warm glow came from the inns and taverns along the seafront. The captain heard the merry sound of fiddles being played and songs being sung – pirate songs he had known since he was a nipper. He saw his crew downing pints of ale and tots of rum in Tortuga's largest inn, the Twelve Daggers.

I'll leave them be for tonight, he thought, and set off down a dark side street.

He found a small, musty tavern that went by the name of The Golden Pig and entered. There were only two other people in the tavern – the bartender, and a woman sitting in a dark corner. The bartender served him a flagon of ale and he took a chair by the dirty window.

He sat there, slowly sipping his drink and reliving his victory. The stroke of luck when the *Doomsday*'s mast had fallen ... the look on the faces of those men as they sank to their death. It was the pinnacle of his life so far.

His thoughts were interrupted by the woman across the tavern. She was saying something. He slammed his flagon down on the table.

'It's a dangerous thing to stop a man's thoughts,' he said fiercely. 'Bite your tongue, or I'll have it on a plate.'

'I have a matter that you must hear of,' she replied evenly from her dark corner, and stared at him in a curious way.

He stared back. This woman, partly concealed by shadow, seemed to be wearing a kind of purple turban.

Jewellery rattled as she lifted an arm to point at him. He knew this type of lowlife – she was a fortune-teller. She had probably heard of his victory that day and intended to rob him of his hard-earned riches through her devious means.

'I am not interested in what you have to offer. I repeat, bite your tongue.'

'I do not want any money for what I am about to tell you,' she said, seeming to read his mind. 'I see your fate stretched out before me. I must warn you that if you set foot on your ship again, you will be in grave danger.'

'Ah, so you have heard of my adventures today. And now you are going to make some story up to strike fear into me. In your profession, customers who fear what you say pay you well. But I warn you, I will not be afraid, whatever you say. You will not get a penny out of me.'

But the woman continued. 'If you return to your ship, it will be sunk by the next full moon.'

Captain Traiton felt a great anger bubbling up inside him. 'One more word out of you and I will not be responsible for my actions!'

'Take my words as you will,' the woman replied. 'But if you ignore them, the next time your ship touches land will be when it is wrecked at the bottom of the sea.'

Captain Traiton stood up, his fists clenched. He had a good mind to shoot the fortune-teller dead there and then.

No, a crueller punishment is more fitting, he thought.

He took hold of the woman by her arm and dragged her out of The Golden Pig. The bartender did not blink an eyelid. Captain Traiton dragged her all the way back to the *Tormenta*. It was surprisingly easy, for she remained silent and did not resist.

There was still a long line of pirates waiting by the ship to be interviewed by the captain's second-in-command.

'Hurry up, Skinner! We set sail for England in the morning.'

Captain Traiton took the woman below deck and locked her in one of the ship's cells.

As he turned the key in the lock she stared at him, expressionless.

'Stop staring at me, or I'll remove both your eyes.'

'You haven't even asked my name,' she said. 'I am Esmeralda.'

'Ha! A suitable name for a fraud like you. Well, Esmeralda, if my ship is destined to sink, then you will go down with us. Perhaps that will change your prediction as to what will happen before the next full moon.'

He walked away and up onto the main deck, feeling the unrelenting stare of the woman on his back.

Really Bad Poetry

'Caspar's taking his time,' said Felix.

Caspar was inside the library, trying to find Capston's poetry book. He'd been happy to go in now it was after school hours.

'Do you really think this Captain Traiton would have sailed the *Tormenta* here to bury some treasure?' asked Drift, sitting next to Felix on the library step. 'Like Albert said, why would a big, old pirate ship come to Thistlewick?'

'Well, isn't it an island in the middle of nowhere, which no one thinks of coming to? It could be the perfect place to hide your treasure.'

The library doors opened and Caspar walked out.

'No luck,' he said.

'Capston's poetry book isn't in the library?' asked Felix.

'It was until half past twelve today. Someone else had the same idea as us.'

'What do you mean?' asked Drift.

'When I couldn't find the book on the shelves, I

asked Mrs Turner about it and she was really surprised. Apparently it hasn't been taken out for fifty years, but today two people have asked for it. Me and—'

'Mr Foxsworth!' Felix realised.

'Yes … he took it out this lunchtime.'

'So that's where he went when I was in detention. I thought he looked distracted when he came back and let me out early.'

Caspar nodded. 'Mr Foxsworth knows more about the *Tormenta* than we thought.'

Felix gritted her teeth as she realised, 'He's had all afternoon to look for clues in Capston's book of poems. He might even know where the treasure is by now.'

'So what do we do?' asked Drift.

'We've got to go back to school and get that book,' Felix replied, her heart pounding.

***

There was no sign of anyone when they arrived at Stormy Cliff School five minutes later. Drift agreed to stay outside while Felix and Caspar attempted to sneak in.

Felix tried the main entrance but it was locked.

'What about the window in the girls' toilets?' Caspar suggested. 'We left that open.'

Felix was pleasantly surprised by how adventurous he was starting to become.

They walked around the side of the building and, sure enough, the window was still ajar. Felix dragged over a nearby bin, climbed up on it and pulled herself in through the window. Caspar followed, arms and legs flailing about, and Felix helped him down. They crept out into the hallway.

'You don't think Mr Foxsworth is still in school, do you?' whispered Caspar.

'I hope not. We'll be careful,' replied Felix.

Outside Mr Foxsworth's office, she took a deep breath and held it as she grabbed hold of the door handle. It turned and the door slowly creaked open to reveal…

An empty office. Felix let out a sigh of relief.

'Quickly, let's find the book. You look on his desk, Caspar.'

Felix went straight over to the bookshelf by the window and started looking through the various folders and books while Caspar searched around the desk.

Before she had made it halfway along a shelf, Caspar exclaimed, 'Aha!'

She turned around to see him pulling a small, old book out of a drawer. 'Nice one, Caspar.'

He put it down on the desk. On the book's faded blue cover, Felix read *My Life in Poems* by Capston Gailsborough.

'See if you can find any poems about stargazing,' she said.

Caspar flicked through the book, reading the titles of the poems far quicker than Felix could keep up with. He stopped at one near the back of the book entitled 'A Startled Stargazer'.

'It looks like this is the poem Capston wrote about seeing the *Tormenta*,' said Caspar.

where is this?

While stargazing one night in my favourite spot
I got a terrible fright that scared me a lot
A large pirate ship on the horizon did appear
As it sailed close to shore, in my heart I felt fear…

'Albert was right,' said Caspar. 'Capston's poems really are bad.'

'That's Mr Foxsworth's writing next to it, isn't it?' Felix pointed. 'He's underlined "my favourite spot" and written "where is this?"'

'Mr Foxsworth's right to underline it. But we already know that clue. We've got to find Capston's secret spot.'

'Does he mention it in any of his other poems?'

Caspar flicked slowly back through the book.

'Hang on, go back to that last one,' said Felix.

Caspar turned the page over to a poem called 'Moonlight'.

The best time to stargaze is always at night

In the place where <u>shark fins</u> dance in the moonlight

'Look, Mr Foxsworth has underlined shark fins. It's a clue about where Capston's stargazing spot was,' said Felix.

'Really? But there have never been sharks in the sea around Thistlewick.' Caspar frowned.

Felix heard a noise – a bird sound – coming from outside. 'What was that?'

She listened again.

Twit-twoo … twit-twoo.

'It's Drift, he's warning us. Someone's coming! Quick, put the book away.'

Caspar threw the book back in the desk drawer and they ducked down behind the desk. A second later, the office door creaked open.

Felix watched through a crack as a tall figure stepped into the office, darkness seeming to follow him in.

'Well, well, well,' Mr Foxsworth boomed. 'First, you failed to write your lines in my detention, Felix Dashwood, then you both thought it was acceptable to run away from school, and now I find you in my office stealing things. You can stop hiding, I know you are in here.'

Felix clenched her fists and slowly stood up, trying to stop herself from being scared by the menacing look in Mr Foxsworth's eyes. Beside her, Caspar was shaking. He'd never been told off by a teacher before.

'We weren't trying to steal anything,' said Felix.

'Do not answer me back! Move away from my desk. Stand against the wall over there.'

Felix and Caspar did as they were told. Felix watched Mr Foxsworth slowly walk over to his desk. He opened the drawer they'd just been looking in, pulled out Capston's book of poems and put it in his trouser pocket.

The head teacher turned back to Felix and Caspar. 'You will both stay here. I am going to fetch your parents. We'll see how they react to finding out they have thieves in their families.'

Felix didn't dare say anything. Mr Foxsworth walked out of the office and slammed the door shut. Felix heard the key turning in the lock and felt a pang of worry.

They were trapped inside Mr Foxsworth's office!

10
Old Sam

Nothing is worse than a rumour aboard a ship in the middle of the ocean.

Five days into their journey back to England and rumours were spreading around the *Tormenta* thick and fast about the strange woman in the turban.

Who was she? Why was she locked up on the ship? She had sat there, day after day, with her eyes closed, muttering quietly to herself.

Captain Traiton stood on the quarterdeck, looking out at the sea, which shone like a newly forged sword, as Skinner filled him in.

'You know how it happens, Captain. The man who keeps the keys to her cell listened to her mutterings. He whispered what he heard to the powder monkeys when they were playing with the rats. They spread the news to the gunners, adding details to the story to make it more dramatic. Over their games of cards, the gunners fought to tell everyone else the tale of the woman below deck and her strange speech. And now the crew are all convinced: we've been cursed by the woman in the turban.'

Captain Traiton turned to his second-in-command. 'I do not believe such superstitious nonsense, and I expect my men to ignore it as well. Keep control of them, Skinner.'

In the five days of their journey so far, they had barely seen a wave, and no other ships had been spotted. The *Tormenta* would have a smooth passage to England, Captain Traiton was sure. He thought again about what Esmeralda had told him about the ship being wrecked by the next full moon, and chuckled to himself. He almost felt sorry for the old crone – her time in the cell would probably do her good.

***

The next day, as Captain Traiton was dozing in his cabin, Skinner ran in. 'Captain, we've a problem.'

He sat bolt upright. 'Where?'

Skinner pointed out to the forecastle. 'It's the crew, Captain.'

Captain Traiton climbed out of his hammock and glared furiously at Skinner. 'I told you to keep control of them!'

He walked out onto the main deck and saw many of the crew gathered by the forecastle. Several of them had swords out. Captain Traiton shook his head. If there was one thing he didn't stand for on his ship it was fighting amongst the crew.

He stormed along the deck and over to them.

'It's happening,' he heard one man cry. 'It's the woman's curse! It's got old Sam!'

Captain Traiton realised that the pirates with their swords out were aiming them at a single pirate – old Sam. He was staggering about, his head rolling, his eyes glazed over. They were trying to push him overboard.

'Get back!' they called. 'Don't touch him!'

'Get him over the side, before the curse spreads!' yelled a gunner.

One of the pirates lunged forwards with his sword, sending old Sam flailing backwards into the railings.

Captain Traiton ripped through the rabble of men. 'Belay that! Put your swords down!'

'I knew it!' said another man in great panic. 'Didn't I warn you this would happen? We're all cursed! We're all dead!'

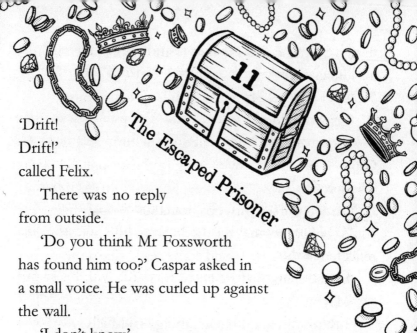

11

The Escaped Prisoner

'Drift! Drift!' called Felix.

There was no reply from outside.

'Do you think Mr Foxsworth has found him too?' Caspar asked in a small voice. He was curled up against the wall.

'I don't know.'

'Do you think Mr Foxsworth knows we've been trying to find the treasure?'

'I don't know, Caspar.' She sat down beside him. 'But now we're locked in here, we might as well try to work out what Capston meant when he wrote about the shark fins.'

Caspar started to rock back and forth. 'What's my mum going to say? She'll be really angry.'

'Come on, Caspar, don't think about that now. Help me figure Capston's poem out.'

Caspar sniffed loudly. 'I suppose it could be a metaphor.'

'What's that?' asked Felix.

'You use metaphors in poems to compare two

things. So you could say that Drift is a pig when he eats his lunch.'

'I get it. Like, Mr Foxsworth is an evil dragon.'

Caspar nodded.

'So what does that make shark fins, and why did Capston say they were dancing in the moonlight?' Felix wondered.

Casper pursed his lips together thoughtfully. 'He could be describing the light from the moon being reflected in the sea around some really sharp rocks.'

'So the shark fins are sharp rocks?'

'Maybe.'

'I think you're onto something,' said Felix.

Remembered the map on the wall high above the table she always sat at during detentions, Felix got up. She climbed onto the table and stood on her toes, just about able to lift down the golden-framed map.

She took it over to Mr Foxsworth's desk. The black and white map showed all the houses in the south of Thistlewick, the Forest of Shadows at the centre and the farms in the north. The sea was represented around the island by various cartoon waves.

'Come and help me look, Caspar. We're looking for a part of the sea around north Thistlewick that has lots of rocks.'

Caspar pushed himself up slowly. 'Is the map accurate, though? And, anyway, there are loads of rocks in the sea on this map. Look.'

He pointed at various points on the map where rocks popped out of the sea.

'But they look nothing like shark fins,' said Felix. She ran a finger around the north of Thistlewick. 'Aha!'

Felix stopped her finger at a small cove, which was surrounded by a semicircle of sharp, triangular rocks.

'That has to be it. The "place where shark fins dance in the moonlight". That is where Capston used to go stargazing.'

'Yes! I'll make a copy of the map,' said Caspar, his eyes brighter now.

He grabbed a pencil and Mr Foxsworth's notepad from the desk, drew a quick sketch and labelled it 'Shark Fin Cove'.

'We'd better put this map back up on the wall, before Mr Foxsworth comes back,' said Felix.

She lifted it off the desk and started to carry it back across the room.

'Hang on, Felix, what's that caught in the back of the frame?' Caspar pulled something out.

'That's just some old newspaper,' said Felix. 'It's probably been there for years. Come on, help me put the map back up.'

'No, look at the date, Felix. It's only from a couple of months ago. Mr Foxsworth must have hidden it there.'

Felix put the map down and watched Caspar unfold the newspaper. It turned out there were two articles.

They looked at the one dated three months before,

from an English newspaper, with the headline: **THIEF TRAITON'S TRIAL ENDS**. It briefly explained that, after being arrested for stealing a large sum of money at gunpoint from a bank, a man named Tristan Traiton had been sentenced to ten years in prison in England. Apparently, he had been on the run from the police for several years and had carried out many such armed robberies. All he had said to the judge after hearing his sentence was, 'That money should have been mine!'

There was a photo with the article, taken from behind and showing a bald man being led to prison by two policemen.

Felix looked at the photo closely. 'There's a giant letter T on the back of his neck – like a tattoo or something.'

'Do you recognise that name, though?' asked Caspar.

'Yes!' Felix realised. 'Traiton was the name of the *Tormenta*'s captain. But he was alive hundreds of years ago.'

'Maybe this Traiton is a relative of Captain Traiton. Mr Foxsworth must have been doing some research into the Traiton family.'

'What's in the second article?' asked Felix.

Caspar opened it up to reveal the large headline: **Traiton's Triumph: Prisoner Escapes**. But it was the photo underneath that caught Felix's attention. It was a mugshot of Tristan Traiton staring straight at the camera, and there was something odd about him. He might not have long, black hair, but his dark eyes looked stern and evil, and his eyebrows curled up.

Felix turned to Caspar, eyes wide. 'I think Tristan Traiton is Mr Foxsworth. They're the same person!'

Caspar nodded slowly. 'You're right… So our head teacher was in prison in England.'

'That's why he's changed his name,' Felix realised. 'There's no way he'd get a job as a head teacher after being in prison. It must be why he's grown his hair so long too – to cover up the tattoo on his neck.'

'Either that or he's wearing a wig,' said Caspar. 'But, Felix, Tristan Traiton was sentenced to ten years in prison. That was only two months ago. But look at the headline – "Prisoner Escapes"; he escaped from prison a month ago and became our head teacher about a week later.'

Felix shook her head, barely able to believe what she was hearing. 'What does it say in the article?'

Caspar read it out.

Just a couple of months ago, Tristan Traiton was sent to prison for the theft of several hundred thousand pounds. He was not supposed to have seen the outside world for ten years. But today it has been confirmed, by a source from the prison service, that Traiton escaped from Pucklebury Prison yesterday night in mysterious circumstances.

'I locked him in his cell last night, but when I came to check on him this morning, he was gone,' prison officer Bert Chalk told this paper. 'There was no sign of how he got out. No bars were broken, no tunnels had been dug. We simply do not know how he did it.'

The police have asked that anyone who sees a man matching Tristan Traiton's description contact them immediately.

'Judging by the skill he showed in escaping from Pucklebury, one of the most secure prisons I know of, Traiton could be anywhere right now,' says Chief Inspector Claxton. 'I would warn any citizens who do see him not to confront this dangerous criminal. Instead, call the police straight away.'

At the time of writing this article, the so called 'dangerous criminal' has not been seen by anyone. We will keep you updated with any developments in the mysterious disappearance of the thief, Tristan Traiton.

Felix frowned at the article, still struggling to take it all in.

'Our head teacher is an escaped and dangerous criminal,' she said slowly.

'Whose real name is Tristan Traiton,' said Caspar.

'And that's why he's after the *Tormenta*'s treasure. Like you said, he must be related to Captain Traiton.' Felix realised she hadn't breathed properly in minutes. She took several deep breaths. 'We need to get out of here

before Mr Foxsworth – or should I call him Traiton – comes back.'

Caspar nodded. He folded the pieces of newspaper up again and wedged them back into the golden frame. 'I'll put the map back up,' said Felix. 'I don't want him to know we've found out his secret.'

'So how are we going to get out of here?' asked Caspar, as Felix returned the map to the wall.

She looked around the room. 'The door's locked. What about the window?'

Caspar went over and tried to open it. 'That's locked too.'

'Then there's only one thing for it,' said Felix.

'What's that?'

'Move out of the way, Caspar.'

Felix picked up a chair – the chair she had spent many hours sitting on in detentions. She turned its legs towards the window and charged full pelt.

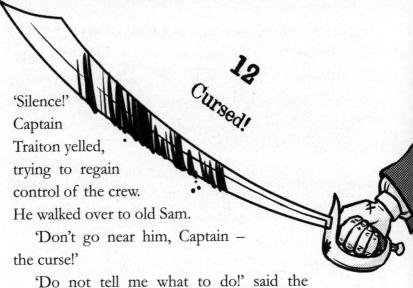

12
Cursed!

'Silence!'
Captain
Traiton yelled,
trying to regain
control of the crew.
He walked over to old Sam.

'Don't go near him, Captain –
the curse!'

'Do not tell me what to do!' said the
captain. He turned to old Sam. 'Straighten yourself
up, man, that's an order.'

But the ragged pirate just swayed back and forth.

Captain Traiton grabbed hold of his neck with both
hands and pulled him close. He sniffed old Sam's breath.
Alcohol. The man reeked of it.

'Put him where he belongs – in the stocks.' He
looked around the confused crew. 'The man is drunk!'

He watched the crew's faces change. They began to
laugh nervously.

'So it's not a curse?' asked the boatswain.

'Curse? Ha! I will say this once and once only. Are
you listening, men? There is no curse. The woman below
deck talks nonsense. I repeat, *there is no curse!* The next man
who even suggests such a thing will be flogged so hard
he won't know what it is to have skin! Am I understood?'

'Aye, Captain,' the crew responded.

Captain Traiton turned and strode down the steps towards the cells, his blood boiling. He rattled the bars of Esmeralda's cell. She sat motionless, not even opening her eyes.

'What have you been saying to my men?'

Now she looked at him and he felt her eyes burning into his mind. She spoke in a deep, mystical voice. 'You will regret capturing this ship. Its treasure is cursed. As long as the *Tormenta*'s treasure is in your possession, you are tied to it. I have seen your fate and that is your curse.'

'I don't believe you,' Captain Traiton spat at her. 'First you tell me this ship will be wrecked before the next full moon, now you tell me that we are cursed by the treasure. I know your game. You are spreading rumours to panic my men. You are trying to gain control of my ship from within your cell.'

'You are the one who chose to lock me in here.'

'Hold your tongue!'

'I will not be silenced,' she said. 'My warning is simple. Rid yourself of your treasure before this ship sinks. As long as you hold onto it, you will be tied to this earth.'

The captain slammed a fist against the bars of her cell in frustration. He swung around and walked over to the keeper of the keys.

'Gather five strong men,' Captain Traiton told him, *'and cut out her tongue!'*

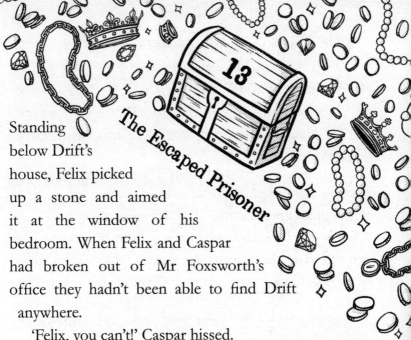

13
The Escaped Prisoner

Standing below Drift's house, Felix picked up a stone and aimed it at the window of his bedroom. When Felix and Caspar had broken out of Mr Foxsworth's office they hadn't been able to find Drift anywhere.

'Felix, you can't!' Caspar hissed.

'We need to see if Drift's at home. I'm only trying to get his attention.'

'You've already broken one window today. Please don't get us into more trouble.'

'Did you hear that?'

'What?'

'Listen,' said Felix.

They stood there in silence and heard shouting coming from the house.

'Tell your mother what you've done,' came Drift's dad's voice.

'I didn't do anything,' Drift replied.

'Don't lie, Drift, Mr Foxsworth has told me all about it.'

'He's lying!' Drift argued back.

'Felix, look,' said Caspar.

'Quiet, Caspar, I'm trying to listen.'

'No, look, this was on the ground.'

He handed Felix a piece of paper with Drift's handwriting on it.

'He must have thrown this out of his bedroom window,' Felix realised.

Drift's writing wasn't great at the best of times, but this was barely readable – it had been written in a rush.

Sorry, I tried to warn you. Mr F found me. He dragged me back home and told my parents I've stolen a load of stuff, so they've shut me up here. Don't go home – I bet Mr F has told your parents the same thing. I think he knows what we're up to. Mr F really is evil. He's asked Dad if he can hire a boat, so looks like he's going to try and find the treasure. Hope you've managed to figure out where the treasure is – you have to find it before him!! I think a boat's a good idea though – you could try getting one. But don't risk going to the harbour. Old Mrs Didsbury's got a boat she never uses. It's in the cove by her cottage – try that.

Dad's coming – G2G – hope u get this!

***

Felix ran up Nettleford Lane on the eastern side of Thistlewick without stopping to catch her breath. The rain from earlier had made the path squelchy, and mud splashed up over Felix's legs, but she didn't care.

She looked back to Caspar, who was struggling along behind her, trying to avoid the puddles.

'Come on, Caspar, nearly there.'

They came to a row of small, thatched cottages. Felix found Mrs Didsbury's and put her nose to the window to see if there was anyone inside. It seemed empty.

Felix beckoned to Caspar and they squeezed down an alleyway along the side of the cottage, past Mrs Didsbury's garden and onto the small area of beach behind it.

'Shouldn't we ask Mrs Didsbury if we can borrow her boat?' Caspar asked in between pants.

'You really think she'd let us? Anyway, there's no time.'

The waves were calm round this side of Thistlewick, and the water gently lapped up and down the beach.

Felix stopped as she saw what she was looking for. Tied up to a wooden post was a small rowing boat.

'Is this Drift's idea of a joke?' asked Caspar. 'No wonder Mrs Didsbury doesn't use it.'

Felix had to admit that, with its peeling paintwork and rotting wood, the boat was in a bad state. But it was their only option. 'It'll be fine.'

'I'm not getting in it. It belongs to Mrs Didsbury,

and even if it did get to Shark Fin Cove without sinking, we'd never get past all those rocks.'

'She won't even notice we've taken it. And it won't sink – don't worry!'

'You've never rowed a boat before. It's too dangerous!'

Their voices got louder as they argued. Felix put a finger to her lips and said in a quieter voice, 'Shhh. If Mrs Didsbury's in her cottage she'll hear us. And it can't be that hard to row…'

Felix heard a door slamming above them.

'Quick, let's get in the boat, there's someone coming.'

Caspar hesitated for a moment. Felix heard the sound of feet on gravel and dragged Caspar down into the boat. They lay flat so as not to be seen.

'Thieves!' a high-pitched voice shouted. 'Thieves! Get out of my boat, I know you are in there. I saw you through my window.'

Felix peeked out of the boat and saw Mrs Didsbury standing over it, her grey hair in a tight bun, a cross look on her face. She was waving a rolling pin threateningly in her hand.

'Well, well. Two children stealing my boat!'

'We weren't stealing it,' said Felix, wishing Drift was here – he could have talked his way out of this. 'We were just borrowing—'

'Your parents will hear of this!' Mrs Didsbury's shrill voice got even higher.

That won't make much difference, Felix thought. *Thanks to*

Tristan Traiton they probably already think we're thieves.

'Explain yourselves!' Mrs Didsbury ordered.

Felix looked to Caspar, but he shook his head. She thought fast.

'We … we heard your boat was in a bad state, so we were going to have a go at repairing it for you. We didn't tell you because we wanted it to be a surprise.'

Mrs Didsbury grabbed hold of Felix's shoulders. She felt herself being lifted out of the boat surprisingly easily – the old woman obviously had more strength than her thin arms suggested. Caspar climbed out and stood next to Felix, his head held low.

'I do not believe you, and even if I did, my boat does not need repairing. I think you should…'

Felix pulled away from Mrs Didsbury's grip and whispered to Caspar, 'Run.'

'What was that?' said Mrs Didsbury. 'No whispering!'

But Felix had scarpered, running off the beach before Mrs Didsbury realised what was going on.

'Sorry,' Felix heard Caspar say before he ran to catch up with her.

They left the old lady standing there, waving her rolling pin in anger.

'Now what do we do?' asked Caspar.

14
Thistlewick Island

The thing many of Captain Traiton's crew feared above all else was a storm. Most of them couldn't swim and, like many captains, this was not something he was willing to teach them, for they might try to escape from his ship if they could. A storm often brought shipwreck, which led to inevitable drowning.

Captain Traiton, however, felt at his best in stormy weather.

As the dark sky set in that night he stood on the forecastle at the very front of the ship and felt the sharp wind cut into him. Clouds fired across the sky at high speed, and through them a bright silver circle of light shone: the full moon.

Since having her tongue cut out, Esmeralda was unable to speak properly and had grown silent. In any case, her warning about the full moon and the curse were now the last things on Captain Traiton's mind. He knew the Spanish navy were after him and he needed to get the *Tormenta* back to England.

The water below was rough, and tossed the ship to

and fro. The captain breathed in the icy spray as his men worked hard to keep the *Tormenta* on a steady course.

'There's a storm brewing, Captain,' said Skinner, coming up to him.

'I can see that. The *Tormenta* will weather anything.'

He walked back up to the quarterdeck and ordered a group of sailors to furl the sails before the wind got too strong.

'Sails or not, this wind'll blow us in a north-easterly direction,' Skinner informed the captain.

'Check our position on the map and let me know of any obstacles that might cause us trouble.'

'Aye, Captain.' Skinner took a map from his jacket pocket and squinted at it. 'Looks like we may be heading for an island called Thistlewick. Seems a small place, so it shouldn't do us harm.'

'We'll be careful to steer round it.'

They continued on their bumpy journey as the angry sea grew more restless. Rain now lashed down on the *Tormenta*, drenching the men on deck. Captain Traiton let it soak into him.

'Land ahoy!' shouted a man from the topmast.

The captain opened his telescope and peered through it. He saw the small mass of rock that Skinner had warned him of – Thistlewick Island. They were heading straight for it. A storm was forming at the north of the island. Lightning pierced through black clouds, followed by the rattle of thunder.

'If we're to avoid the island, we'll need to head straight for that storm,' he informed Skinner. 'I'll take the wheel.'

He braced himself for the challenge ahead and used all his force to control the ship. He skilfully steered the *Tormenta* away from land, but quickly found himself in the teeth of the storm.

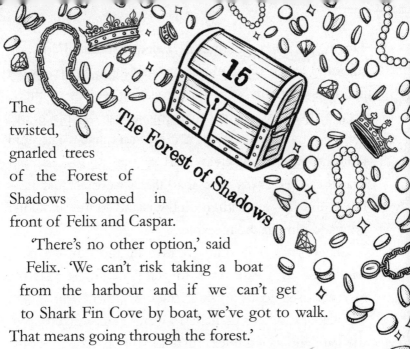

The twisted, gnarled trees of the Forest of Shadows loomed in front of Felix and Caspar.

The Forest of Shadows

'There's no other option,' said Felix. 'We can't risk taking a boat from the harbour and if we can't get to Shark Fin Cove by boat, we've got to walk. That means going through the forest.'

'It's getting late, Felix,' Caspar warned. 'Shouldn't we go home? We can try again in the morning.'

'But if we go home, we'll probably never be allowed out again – not if Tristan Traiton's got us into trouble.'

'Then maybe we should go to the police. Like the newspaper article said, Tristan Traiton is a dangerous criminal.'

'You really think the police would believe us over him? He's managed to convince everyone he's our head teacher, so he's obviously really good at lying. We wouldn't stand a chance. We just have to get to the treasure before he does!'

A tall fence stretched along the length of the forest, to keep people out, or maybe to keep something in.

Throughout her childhood, Felix had heard lots of rumours about what might be inside the forest. Some people said there were human-eating wolves in there, bigger than any man; others reckoned the place was haunted by evil spirits; Farmer Potts had once said that the trees themselves tried to trap people in their branches. Felix was sure that these were all just tales made up to scare children on the island so they wouldn't go wandering in the forest.

There was only one entrance in and out – a gate, which led to a safe track through the forest that the farmers used to bring their tractors down from north Thistlewick, where their fields were. Felix walked up to the gate and saw a thick, rusty-looking padlock keeping it firmly locked.

She looked up at the fence. It was at least four times the size of her, she guessed, but she felt confident. Felix stepped back a few paces to give herself a bit of a run up, then leapt towards the gate. She hung on to the wire mesh, using the gaps between it as hand- and footholds, and slowly climbed up. She got to halfway and stopped to catch her breath.

'You might make it over, but I won't,' Caspar called up to her.

'We can worry about that in a minute,' said Felix, and continued her climb.

As she neared the top, she lifted her arm up to get another handhold and felt a sharp stabbing pain in the palm of her hand. She looked up and realised that the top of the gate was covered in barbed wire. She loosened her grip, but her other hand slipped and she fell backwards. Before she knew what had happened she hit the ground hard.

Caspar ran over. 'Felix! Are you OK?'

She lay there for a few seconds staring up at the darkening sky. Then she shook her head. 'Fine.'

'Look at your hand, Felix.'

She did and saw it was bleeding from where the barbed wire had stuck into it.

'OK, so that probably wasn't a good idea.' Felix felt around in her bag, found a tissue, and wiped away the blood. 'Well, we might not be able to get over the gate, but this fence is ancient. There must be a hole in it somewhere that we can squeeze through.'

Felix wandered off along the edge of the forest, determined not to give up. She hadn't even gone a hundred metres before she found what she was looking for.

'Come here, Caspar!'

She lay down and started pulling brambles and weeds away from the bottom of the fence. Caspar joined in and they quickly revealed a small hole in the wire of the fence. Felix squeezed through easily enough and stood up inside the Forest of Shadows.

Caspar crouched down and stared through the hole.

'You can do it, Caspar.'

'But if we go through here we won't know where the safe track is,' he said.

'It's only just over there on the left. We'll find it easily enough.'

Before Caspar had a chance to complain, Felix grabbed hold of his hand and pulled him through the hole into the forest.

They looked ahead of them. Even here at the forest's edge, the trees were thick and Felix could hardly see through them.

'I don't suppose you've got a torch?' asked Caspar.

Felix shook her head. 'We'll just have to find our way to the safe track in the dark. You're not scared of the dark, are you?'

'No,' said Caspar.

'Well that must be about the only thing you're not scared of.'

'Oi!'

They set off, feeling their way around the trees. Felix had her hands out in front of her to brush low-lying branches out of the way. She knew they needed to head left to get to the safe track, but the trees on their left were too thick and close together to get past, so they crept forwards into further darkness until they found a break in the trees, then they turned left.

Though Felix couldn't see her feet, she could hear them as they stepped over dead leaves and branches, which rustled and cracked loudly.

This was definitely creepy.

'You OK?' she asked Caspar.

'Yes,' he said in a small voice. 'I think we need to turn left.'

'We just did.'

'No, I mean left again.'

They did so and kept going. It was difficult to tell how long they had been walking for, but Felix had the feeling that they should have found the safe track by now. The trees were only getting more packed together, though, and the smell around them – of mud and rotting wood – was getting stronger.

'Let's try heading right,' Felix suggested, starting to get anxious.

But that didn't help either – just more and more trees, each one rougher than the last.

'Felix, we have to face it. We're lost!' Caspar stopped dead in his tracks. Felix stopped too and turned to face him. 'It's late, and my mum will be so worried. We're lost in the Forest of Shadows and we don't really know where we're meant to be going anyway!'

'We're trying to get to Shark Fin Cove.'

'But we're only guessing where that is based on Albert's story and a couple of poems. We don't even know if the *Tormenta*'s treasure will be there and, if it is, what if it's dangerous to get to?'

'Breathe, Caspar, calm down,' said Felix in a gentle voice. It seemed that the forest was bringing out all of

Caspar's worries at once. 'We're on an adventure, and adventures are exciting and unknown. Anyway, this is important. We're doing this to keep you on Thistlewick, remember? That's why we need to get to the treasure before Tristan Traiton does.'

Caspar slowly nodded, but he didn't look convinced.

Felix tried again. 'How does your mum feel about having to leave Thistlewick?'

'She hates it,' admitted Caspar. 'She's been crying a lot ever since she lost her job. She loves living here. We both do.'

'Then think about your mum. We're doing this for her.'

'OK,' said Caspar, sounding more confident now.

They both heard a sound then. A sound that made Felix's heart turn to ice. A long, menacing howl echoing around the trees.

Were the stories about wolves living in the forest true?

'We need to keep moving. It doesn't matter where. We're not safe if we stand still.'

Felix set off, almost running, not caring about tripping over the dead branches on the ground. For once, Caspar kept up with her.

She looked up into the tree canopy and saw faint glimmers of light shining through. It didn't help her to see any better, though – the light just created lots of shadows, which danced around the forest. Suddenly the trees seemed ten times taller. The shadows of their branches really did look like ancient hands reaching down to grab Felix and Caspar.

'I can see why they call it the Forest of Shadows,' said Caspar, and let out a nervous laugh.

Felix's mind spun. She couldn't see where she was going any more. Then her left leg got stuck under something – probably a log. She tried to pull it away and tripped, landing flat on her face on the forest floor. The smell of rot was almost unbearable. A tidal wave of creepy-crawlies started to climb all over her. She swept them away and pushed herself up to standing.

She heard a noise from the trees. A fluttering of wings. Hundreds of them.

'It's the birds, Felix,' said Caspar. 'They're flying away. Whatever scared them must be close.'

Another howl rang out through the trees, much louder this time. Much closer.

Felix shook her head and started to see things around her properly again. Ahead she spotted a grassy patch covered in golden light.

'Look, a clearing. Let's head for that!'

'Felix…' Caspar said slowly, gripping hold of her. 'There's a shadow moving towards us.'

'It's OK, Caspar, it's just the tree branches.'

'That's no tree branch – look!'

Felix turned and saw what Caspar meant. The shadows of the trees kept swirling around, making weird patterns, but through all this came a different shadow altogether. Pure black, with a very clear shape. The shape of a wolf! But not like any of the wolves Felix had seen on TV – judging by its shadow, it was bigger than a human.

'The rumours are true,' she whispered.

She couldn't make out any features on the creature, but she heard it growling and spitting as it edged closer to them.

Caspar was gasping with fear.

'Don't make a sound,' Felix said through gritted teeth. 'Stay calm and copy me.'

Her heart beating faster than it ever had before, she started to edge slowly backwards, pulling Caspar with her.

Every step they took, the black, faceless creature seemed to take one too. But its steps were longer than theirs – it was gaining on them, and as it did it got bigger, towering above them.

The wolf's snarls rang in Felix's ears. She couldn't help staring at it as she and Caspar kept moving backwards. She could just make out razor-like teeth protruding from the creature's huge mouth.

She looked quickly behind her – there was nothing there that would help. If they ran, the wolf would catch them easily. What could she do?

But it was too late. Suddenly the creature leapt straight at them.

They both screamed.

Felix lost her footing and fell backwards.

She kept on falling, into a never-ending pit of darkness.

16 The Storm

Waves swept over the *Tormenta* like the tentacles of a giant octopus, dragging the pirates to all four corners before rising up to attack again. A thick mist started to form around Captain Traiton at the wheel, swirling like a tornado. The ship hit a swell of water and lurched sideways.

'Rocks ahead, Captain. We're not safe yet.'

'I know, Skinner. I'll take us round them.'

Captain Traiton squinted through the mist and saw the group of sharp, jagged rocks in front of him, sticking out of the water like shark fins. He knew each one would rip a hole in the ship greater than any cannonball.

A sudden flash of lightning exploded over Captain Traiton's head, momentarily blinding him. As it cleared, he felt something jump at his back. He looked over his shoulder and saw the wild hair and crazed grin of Esmeralda. She reached around his neck, her fingers squeezing at his throat with surprising strength. Her mad eyes were wide open and she spat blood as she tried to speak through her tongue-less mouth.

'Cuuuurse!' she managed to get out, in a voice barely

audible above the storm. *'Cuuuurse you!'*

Captain Traiton took his hands off the wheel and grabbed hold of her. He threw her to the deck and she crumpled into a heap like a rag doll.

'Get her below deck! Lock her in irons!' he yelled, looking around the crew. 'Whoever is responsible for letting her out will pay for it when we've got through this storm!'

'Captain!' Skinner shouted. 'CAPTAIN!'

'WHAT?'

Captain Traiton looked ahead again, just in time to see the large rock directly in front of the *Tormenta*. Too late, he grabbed the wheel and pulled it sideways with all his might.

17

The Hole

Felix opened her eyes. She stared up at the tree canopy far, far away.

In a way it was a good job the huge hole had been there, she decided. They had fallen into it just as the wolf was about to attack. It had been a painful fall, she guessed around ten metres down, but it had saved them from the creature outside.

Felix could hear the wolf above them now, growling down. She huddled up next to Caspar, her heart beating fast, and waited. The wolf let out a high-pitched howl. Then there was silence.

'Has it gone?' asked Caspar after a minute.

'I think so.'

She stood up stiffly and looked at the muddy walls of the hole around her. She tried to grip hold of one of the sides, but the mud just gave way beneath her fingers.

'There's no way we can climb out.'

She thought for a minute about what else they could do.

Felix tipped back her head. 'Help! Help! We're trapped down here.'

'That's not going to work,' said Caspar. 'No one comes in the forest, so there's no one to hear us.'

Felix sat down, suddenly feeling quite dizzy. It was probably a delayed reaction from the fall.

Caspar put a hand on her shoulder. 'You need to rest.'

'We don't have time. We have to get out. We need to get to … to the…' Her head was swimming, her vision blurry.

'Lie down, just for a bit. You don't look well.'

Felix was barely aware of what Caspar was doing, but the next thing she realised he was helping her to lie down and rest on her coat as a pillow. The dirt this far under the forest floor was actually quite warm, compared to the freezing cold of the forest above. Felix felt her eyelids closing and let herself drift off.

***

Felix blinked awake.

Although it still seemed as dark as it had been the last time she had opened her eyes, it felt like she had been asleep for hours.

She looked over to Caspar, who was gently snoring. Everything they were meant to be doing flooded back to her.

Felix tapped Caspar but he didn't stir, so she tried shaking his shoulder. Caspar's eyes flickered open.

'Hello,' he croaked.

'What's the time?' asked Felix.

Caspar squinted at his watch. 'Eight.'

'In the morning?'

'Yep.'

Felix groaned. 'We've been asleep all night! Tristan Traiton's probably found the treasure by now and we're still stuck in the Forest of Shadows. It's too late.'

Caspar frowned, then called out, 'Help!'

'I thought you said that wouldn't work,' said Felix.

'Well, I don't have any better ideas and, whether we're too late to get the treasure or not, we need to get out of here.'

They both shouted out for a minute or so at the top of their voices, hoping that a miracle would happen and someone would hear them.

'We should have thought ahead before we came into the forest,' said Caspar. 'We didn't even bring a torch.'

'Ow!' Felix shouted, putting her hand to her head.

'What happened?' asked Caspar.

'Something just whacked me.'

She felt around to see what it was and found a piece of rope dangling down.

'Look, Caspar, rope. It *is* a miracle! Hello? Is there someone up there?'

Torchlight shone on them from above and they heard a voice call down, 'The rope's tied to a tree. Climb up it one at a time.'

It was so distorted by the echo of the hole that Felix couldn't tell who it belonged to.

'You don't think it's Tristan Traiton, do you?' asked Caspar.

'I don't know.' She called up, 'Who is it?'

There was a slight pause, then the voice responded, 'It's Drift.'

Felix grinned at Caspar and grabbed hold of the rope. 'I'll go first and see if the rope's safe.'

It took her weight. Gripping the rope with both hands and pressing her feet against the side of the hole, she pulled herself up. As she reached the edge of the hole, Drift rushed forward to help lift her up.

'Drift!' She grinned and put her arms around her friend in excitement.

'Er … hi, Felix,' he said, awkwardly accepting her hug.

'How on earth did you find us?'

'Let's get Caspar out first. I'll explain everything later.'

'Caspar,' Felix called down the hole. 'Grab hold of the rope and we'll pull you up.'

'OK, I'm holding the rope,' came Caspar's echoed voice.

Felix and Drift grabbed hold of their end of the rope and started pulling. Caspar was surprisingly heavy and it took them a few tugs before they made any progress. As he got nearer to the surface, it became easier. They pulled him out and he stood up next to them.

'Thank you,' he said with a small smile. 'Hi, Drift.'

Drift nodded to him and loosened the rope from where he'd tied it round a nearby tree. 'How exactly did you two end up down that hole?'

'We got lost in the forest last night,' Felix explained.

'You came into the Forest of Shadows last night?' Drift frowned. 'How long have you been down that hole?'

'All night,' Felix admitted. 'We were walking through the forest and it got darker and darker and we couldn't find the safe path. Then this huge creature started chasing us. You know the rumours about there being wolves in this forest, Drift? I think they're true. This wolf creature was about to attack us when we fell down the hole.'

'That's freaky,' said Drift. 'I can't believe you've been in here all night, though. I thought your parents would have kept you locked up until this morning like mine did. Didn't Mr Foxsworth drag you home yesterday when we got caught?'

'No, I smashed a window in his office and we escaped before he brought our parents to fetch us,' Felix explained.

Drift raised his eyebrows, clearly impressed.

'But how did you know we were in the forest, Drift?' asked Caspar.

'Before you answer, shall we keep walking?' Felix suggested. 'Just in case any more wolves turn up. Any idea how to get to the north from here, Drift?'

Drift pulled a compass out of his bag and held it in front of him. The needle on the compass pointed behind them, so they set off in that direction.

'I snuck out as soon as Mum and Dad went to work,' Drift explained. 'I went to your houses but there was no one around, so I went to see if Mrs Didsbury's boat was gone and she came straight out of her cottage and started yelling at me, saying you two had tried to steal it yesterday. So I guessed that without a boat you must have tried coming through the forest.'

Drift looked at his compass again and they turned slightly left to keep heading north.

'I decided that I might as well come the same way, and that I might find you – either in here or at the north of the island. I ran home and fetched my camping gear from the shed, then I set off into the forest. After a while, I heard you shouting.'

'We're lucky you did!' said Felix. 'I was starting to think we'd be stuck down there forever. As it is, our evil head teacher is bound to have got to the treasure already, if he hired a boat from your dad last night like you said in your note.'

'Maybe not. He tried to hire a boat, but they were all out,' Drift explained. 'But Dad mentioned that Mr Foxsworth has hired one for this morning.'

'So he hasn't found the treasure yet!' A huge wave of relief flowed through Felix – they still had a chance.

'But it won't take him long in a boat if he's figured out that the treasure's in Shark Fin Cove,' said Caspar.

'Shark Fin Cove?' asked Drift.

'Yes, it's where Capston's stargazing spot was,' explained Felix. 'And that's not the only thing we've found out. Mr Foxsworth isn't his real name.'

'He's an escaped criminal called Tristan Traiton,' said Caspar.

'Traitor Traiton, more like,' said Felix.

'I'm not sure if traitor is the right word,' said Caspar. 'But he did lie about being a real head teacher.'

'Well, that's what I'm calling him from now on.'

'Traiton?' Drift frowned. 'Isn't that…'

'The name of the *Tormenta*'s captain, yes. Traitor Traiton is his great-great-great-great-grandson, or something,' said Felix.

Drift raised his eyebrows. 'Wow! An escaped criminal disguising himself as a head teacher so he can find pirate treasure. He really is evil. Does he know that you know all this?'

'I don't think so,' said Felix.

Caspar's eyebrows knitted together in concern. 'Can you imagine how angry he'll be if he does find out we know his real secret. He was sent to prison for armed robbery. Who knows what he'll do to us.'

'We just have to get to the treasure before him,' said Felix, striding on and feeling more determined than ever.

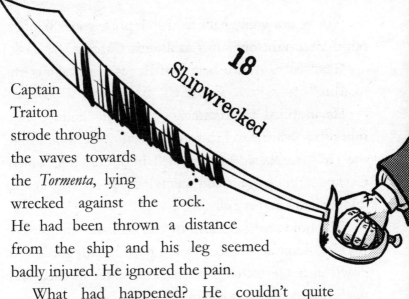

18
Shipwrecked

Captain
Traiton
strode through
the waves towards
the *Tormenta*, lying
wrecked against the rock.
He had been thrown a distance
from the ship and his leg seemed
badly injured. He ignored the pain.

What had happened? He couldn't quite remember, but the results were devastating. The *Tormenta* was on its side, half submerged in water like the carcass of a sea monster. The ship's masts had been snapped clean off and large chunks of wood were being tossed around in the waves.

Around him, Captain Traiton heard the cries and groans of his injured crew.

'Skinner!' he called. 'Skinner, are you alive?'

He found his second-in-command helping a pirate with a bad gash in his arm off the ship.

'Skinner, organise the men and make for land!' he commanded. 'Those who can walk must carry those who can't.'

He walked on, taking in mouthfuls of salty water as it smashed into his face, his mind focused on one thing.

'You're not going back to the ship, are you?' Skinner called after him. 'She's lost to the sea, Captain.'

'The sea can have her now. But it's not taking my treasure!'

He grabbed two gunners, who were limping but otherwise unhurt, and instructed them to help him find the treasure chest. They waded into the ship, which creaked ominously around them. It could collapse at any minute and kill them all.

The hold at the bottom of the ship was completely flooded. Captain Traiton took a deep breath and dived down into the ice-cold water. The water swelled and pushed into him and he had to fight against it. He saw the large hole in the wood where the rock had struck through – the last thing he wanted was to get swept through it and out to sea.

It didn't take him long to find the chest. It was lying under a pile of rope on the sea bed. He swept the rope away, but the chest was a dead weight and he couldn't lift it. He needed air – and more hands. He swam back up to where the two gunners were waiting for him. They all dived down.

The gunners grabbed a handle each and Captain Traiton somehow wedged his arms under the chest. With sheer determination they forced it up off the sea bed. As it reached the surface of the water the chest felt a lot heavier. One of the gunners' hands slipped and the chest crashed down onto Captain Traiton's arm. He felt the pain shoot through him but refused to show it and gritted his teeth.

'Be careful, man!'

The gunner grabbed hold of the chest again and, between them, the three men pushed it back through the ship as the water rose quickly around them. As they passed by the gun deck, Captain Traiton saw Esmeralda tied up in her cell, her hands tugging desperately at the bars. She had given up trying to talk and was wailing a long, deathly cry.

'What about the woman?' asked one of the gunners. 'Should we save her?'

'No!' Captain Traiton said viciously. 'The treasure is more important. We leave her here to drown!'

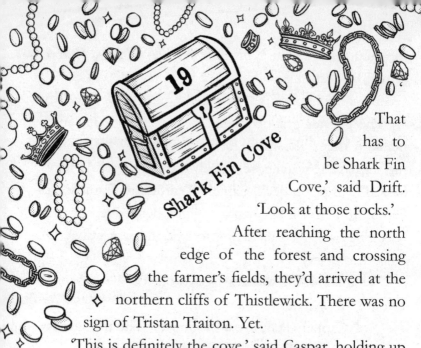

Shark Fin Cove

That
has to
be Shark Fin
Cove,' said Drift.
'Look at those rocks.'

After reaching the north edge of the forest and crossing the farmer's fields, they'd arrived at the northern cliffs of Thistlewick. There was no sign of Tristan Traiton. Yet.

'This is definitely the cove,' said Caspar, holding up his map alongside the view in front of them.

'So we're standing in the same spot that Capston did when he was stargazing,' said Felix.

From the top of the cliff, she looked down at the view. It reminded her of one of the postcards that were sold in the post office. The sky was crystal blue, with only one cloud floating in it like the feather of a giant seagull. The horizon was clearly visible and the sun shone powerfully over the sea, making it shimmer in rich golden colours. The only sound Felix could hear was the deep hum of the waves and the occasional gull cry from up above.

Even though the water was quite calm, Felix could tell how dangerous Shark Fin Cove was. Thick, granite-grey rocks circled the cove, stretching far out to sea: big ones, small ones, wide and thin, all tightly packed together and all a sharp, triangular shape. Felix could definitely understand why Capston had described them as shark fins. She thought back to Capston's story about the *Tormenta* coming near this cove. Captain Traiton really must have been mad to have brought his ship so close to these rocks.

'How exactly are we going to get down there?' asked Caspar. He was looking at the huge drop from the top of the cliff to the small area of sandy cove below.

'It's too big a drop to use my rope. We'll have to climb down,' said Drift.

Caspar's eyes widened with worry. 'Oh, great.'

Felix patted him on the shoulder. 'It's OK, Caspar, just follow what I do. Place your hands and feet exactly where I put mine and you'll be fine.'

Caspar looked at her with raised eyebrows, clearly showing that he thought he would be anything but fine.

Drift turned to Felix. 'I'll race you.'

Felix shrugged. 'The quicker we get down there the better.'

'This is not a time for racing!' Caspar said anxiously.

But Felix and Drift had already climbed over the top of the cliff and were starting to make their way down. Above her, Felix saw Caspar take a big gulp of breath. He edged his way over to the edge of the cliff and slowly lowered his feet onto the rock face.

'That's it, Caspar,' she called. 'Put your left foot on that bit of rock sticking out there.'

Once she was sure Caspar was doing OK, Felix looked down. Drift was already at least a metre below her. She began moving her arms and legs at top speed.

They had climbed down plenty of cliffs before, but never one as big as this. It wouldn't be too hard, though – the rock was really jagged and lumpy, which meant there were loads of hand- and footholds. Felix concentrated hard, placing her right foot in a gap, then moving her left arm down to support her weight against a bit of rock sticking out. By the time Felix was halfway down, she was at least a metre ahead of Drift.

She looked up to Caspar again. He hadn't moved far and seemed to be frozen in an odd position. His legs were nearly doing the splits.

'You alright, Caspar?'

'I'm … I'm stuck. I can't…' His voice trailed off.

'Wimp,' Felix heard Drift say under his breath.

'You're closer to him, Drift. Go and help him,' she said.

'No way. I'm not helping,' Drift replied, and continued climbing downwards.

Felix looked up at Caspar again. A bit of rock crumbled from under his left foot, which skidded across the rock face. His feet were dangling in mid-air, his hands the only thing stopping him from falling as he clung on desperately to the rock.

'Aaahhh!' Caspar cried out.

Felix quickly clambered back up the cliff. Once she'd reached Caspar, she balanced herself, grabbed hold of his legs and guided them to find some footholds. She stayed alongside him, slowly helping him find his way down the cliff. His arms were trembling and, although he didn't say a word, he was breathing in and out really quickly.

After what seemed like a very long time they eventually jumped the last metre to the thick, golden sand. Caspar sat down and leant against the bottom of the cliff, wheezing.

Felix spotted Drift at the edge of the water. She leapt up and stormed over to him.

'Well I clearly beat you,' said Drift.

'That wasn't nice, Drift! Caspar could have fallen. He could have died.'

'Yeah, well, he didn't, did he?'

Drift picked up a rock and skimmed it across the water. It bounced three times against the surface and disappeared with a plop.

'Just remember why we're here, Drift,' said Felix. 'We're trying to find this treasure for Caspar. I wish you two would get on better!'

She looked around Shark Fin Cove. There were no footprints in the sand other than theirs, no boats in the water and no sign that any other living being – human or animal – had been here.

'It looks like we've made it before Traitor Traiton,' Felix said with relief. 'But we'd better be quick. He could turn up at any minute, especially if he has a boat.'

Drift picked up another stone and this time lobbed it a long way out. It hit one of the rocks, bounced off it and landed in the water with a splash.

'Any idea where the treasure's buried?' He turned round to face Felix and added sarcastically, 'I can't see any Xs round here.'

'It could be anywhere, really,' replied Felix.

'We'd better get digging then,' said Drift. 'But how exactly are you planning to dig?'

'I don't know,' admitted Felix. 'Maybe we could find a sharp bit of rock.'

'Or we could use this.'

Drift took a shovel out of his rucksack. At first it looked really small, but Drift pulled at the handle and it extended into a full-sized shovel.

'Good thinking,' said Felix.

'Might as well start here,' said Drift, and he plunged the spade into the sand.

'What was that?' asked Caspar, walking over to join Felix and Drift.

'What?' asked Felix.

Then she heard it too. A noise that made all three of them clutch their hands to their ears. It was the loudest, most piercing scream Felix had ever heard.

'I think it's coming from the sea,' she yelled, her

hands still over her ears.

Felix shook her head, trying to get the sound out of it, but it just became more high-pitched.

'What is it?' asked Drift.

'It's probably some poor sea creature you hit with that stone, Drift,' said Caspar.

As quickly as the sound had started it stopped.

'Thank goodness for that,' said Felix, lowering her hands.

Drift started digging again.

'You do realise that pirates didn't usually bury their treasure on beaches, don't you?' said Caspar.

'What do you mean?' Drift stopped digging and glared at him.

'That just happens in stories. In reality, pirates usually tried to hide their treasure in a cave.'

'Well, there are loads of caves.'

Felix scanned the cliff face. Drift was right. To one end of Shark Fin Cove there was a big pile of rocks against the cliff, and the rest of the cliff face was full of holes and cracks that might be caves.

'Which one's the treasure in, genius?' asked Drift.

'I don't know,' Caspar replied. 'We need to have a look inside them all.'

Drift rolled his eyes. 'Obviously.'

'Right, less arguing, more looking,' said Felix. 'Traitor Traiton could be here at any minute, remember?' She strode back towards the cliff at the eastern side of the cove. The other two caught her up. 'We'll start this side and work our way along.'

The first gap in the cliff was a wide one and they all fitted inside easily. It was hardly a cave though – they had only walked a few metres in before they came to a solid rock wall. The next few gaps in the cliff were too small to fit through.

Felix spotted one hole that was very low down on the cliff. She laid flat on her stomach and slithered her way inside it. To her surprise, when she was all the way through, she was able to stand up. She looked upwards and saw a circle of light high above.

'This isn't a cave,' Felix called. 'It's a giant hole in the cliff that goes all the way to the top, like a chimney.'

Drift helped to pull her back out again and they continued their search.

Gap by gap, crack by crack, they looked into everything that they thought might be a cave, but with no luck.

Felix ran her hand through her hair, frustrated. 'We don't have time for this.'

'I'm not sure if they would have chosen a cave that was so obvious, anyway,' said Caspar. 'They'd find one that was hard to spot.'

'OK.' Felix scanned along the cliff face and came to the large collection of rocks piled up at the other end of the cliff. 'What about behind those rocks, then?'

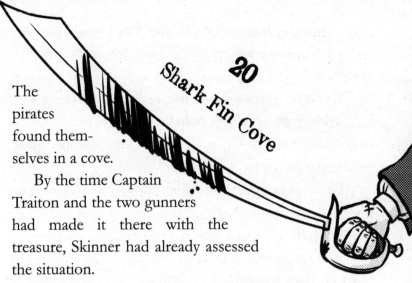

Shark Fin Cove

The pirates found themselves in a cove.

By the time Captain Traiton and the two gunners had made it there with the treasure, Skinner had already assessed the situation.

'Looks like the only way out of this cove is to climb the cliffs, Captain.'

Captain Traiton looked upwards. In the darkness, he could barely see the mass of rock stretching into the heavens, but it looked like it went at least a hundred feet up. In this weather, with so many of the crew injured, there was no way they could make it to the top. He sensed the pain in his left leg growing and reached down. It felt sticky. Sure enough, when he lifted his hand up, he saw it was covered in blood. Not even he could scale the cliffs with a damaged leg.

The seawater was swelling up around the pirate crew. Soon it would cover the entire cove and drown them like rats.

Some of the pirates were starting to panic. 'We're trapped!' they called. 'Doomed! Cursed!'

'Enough!' bellowed the captain, but he could not

shut the worry from his mind now. How would they get out of this wretched place? 'There has to be another way.'

'Captain!' a pirate called from near the cliffs.

'What is it? Speak up, man.'

'A gap in the cliff. A cave. It goes a fair distance back. We're saved!'

There were cheers of relief. Captain Traiton walked over – there was indeed a large slit in the hard rock, only just wide enough for a man to get through.

'Arrange light,' he ordered. 'We'll head in and see just how far back it goes.'

Once torches had been lit, the pirate crew filed in through the gap, Captain Traiton leading the way, the treasure carried closely behind him by the two gunners.

They found themselves in a long, snaking tunnel. It seemed to go on for miles and Captain Traiton's injured leg soon got tired. He was relieved when they came to a wide, tall cave.

From in here, the storm outside sounded like a distant memory. The pirates collapsed to the ground, exhausted.

'We will stay here until the storm has abated,' Captain Traiton announced. 'Get some rest. We may well be here till morning.'

He sat down next to his treasure and placed his hand over the top of the chest. As his men slept, he kept watch over the cave.

Captain Traiton heard the storm picking up again, blasting outside the cave. He stared at the tunnel, wondering how powerful the waves were now and whether they would find their way through the gap.

Just moments later, the water started rushing in. The icy spray hit the sleeping crew, who jumped up, fear in their eyes. Captain Traiton suppressed any fear he might have felt and watched as the water level got quickly higher and higher.

He tried to think. There was no way out of the cave. The water was blocking the only exit. The crew had checked and the cave did not stretch any further back.

For some reason, an image of Esmeralda appeared in his mind. He thought about what she had said. He did not want to believe in such superstitious claptrap, but she *had* been right about the *Tormenta* being wrecked by the full moon. Did that mean she was also correct about the cursed treasure? If so, then it was hardly a curse. As long as the treasure was his, Captain Traiton and his men would be 'tied to this earth'.

Surely that meant that whatever happened now, whether the sea flooded the cave or not, they would live.

He stood there, feeling powerful and strong, watching the water climb and climb up his body, as the waves kept rushing in.

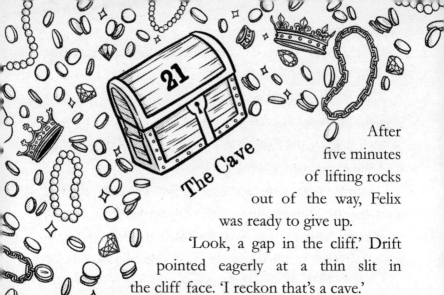

The Cave

After five minutes of lifting rocks out of the way, Felix was ready to give up.

'Look, a gap in the cliff.' Drift pointed eagerly at a thin slit in the cliff face. 'I reckon that's a cave.'

'That can't be a cave,' said Caspar. 'You couldn't fit a pencil through that.'

Felix tried pressing herself into the gap. It was a very tight squeeze and she scraped her hands against the rock, but she made it through.

'Shine your torch in here, Drift.'

He turned it on and shone it past Felix into the darkness. She felt her way back into the cliff and saw a thin tunnel stretching out in front of her.

'Don't go too far, Felix!' said Caspar.

She moved back to the entrance. 'I think this could be it. It's tight, but there's definitely a tunnel. Shall we see where it leads?'

'What are we waiting for?' Drift started pressing himself into the crack to join Felix.

'Hang on,' said Caspar. 'What if we get stuck in there?'

'If you're going to whine so much, you can stay out there in the cove,' said Drift. 'Me and Felix will go and find the treasure without you.'

Felix stared past Caspar and Drift and out to sea. 'What's that on the horizon?'

Drift followed her gaze. 'A boat.'

'It must be Tristan Traiton!' Caspar realised.

'Let's be quick, then,' said Felix. 'Caspar, you're coming in with us. I'm not leaving you out there for Traitor Traiton to find.'

Caspar gritted his teeth. 'OK. But we should put some of these rocks back in place to cover the gap, so that he won't be able to find the cave entrance easily.'

Felix and Drift went back through the gap and helped Caspar pile up rocks.

'Argh!' yelled Drift. 'It's that wailing noise again.'

Felix put her hands over her ears – the noise was even louder than before.

'Quick – there's enough rocks there now,' she said. 'Let's get into the tunnel.'

They all squeezed through the crack. Drift flicked on the torch again and they started to make their way along the tunnel. The rock that surrounded them looked ancient. It was dark and wet and covered in slimy green stuff. Felix's feet slipped on the smooth surface and she pressed her arms firmly against the sides to avoid falling over. At least it was clear where they had to go. There was only one path to follow, straight back into the cliffs.

The wailing from the sea echoed around them. Felix kept wondering what it was – maybe some kind of warning, something trying to stop them going into the cave? She quickly put that thought to the back of her mind and reminded herself why they were here. They had to find the treasure.

The further they went along the tunnel the darker it got, until, even with the light from the torch, they could only see a metre in front of them. The wailing that had filled Felix's ears faded away and a seaweedy smell blocked her nostrils now.

After a few minutes the tunnel widened out enough for Felix and Drift to walk side by side. Felix looked over her shoulder – Caspar was lagging behind by quite a distance, treading very slowly on the slippery rock.

'Don't go too fast, Drift, or Caspar won't have any torchlight.'

'He's really slow,' Drift whispered. 'He's done nothing but hold us up.'

'He was really helpful when we were finding out about the *Tormenta*. We couldn't have done that as quickly without him.'

Drift stared back at Caspar struggling along behind them and shook his head. 'He's pathetic. The biggest adventure he probably had before this was reading a four hundred page book or something.'

'Shut up, Drift! That's better than you could do. You're still learning the alphabet, aren't you?

'A, B, C, D, E, er … what comes after E?' he said in a pretend stupid voice.

Felix glared at him, but she couldn't keep it up. Both of them burst out laughing. Their laugh echoed all around the tunnel, making it sound like there were hundreds of Felixes and Drifts inside.

A sudden gust of wind hit them both in the face. It was so powerful Felix put her hands over her eyes as it whistled past them.

'How can you have wind coming from inside a cave?' asked Drift.

'Don't know. Caspar might.' Felix looked back, but there was no sign of him. 'Where's he gone?'

Drift shrugged.

Felix ran back down the tunnel. 'Caspar?'

She waited a few seconds. There was no reply. Where could he have gone? They were still in one long tunnel with no side exits, so he couldn't exactly have got lost.

'I'll catch you up!' a voice echoed from a distance away.

'He's probably just tying his shoelace or something,' said Drift. 'Let's keep moving.'

Felix frowned and joined Drift again. 'This tunnel is going on forever. I wonder how far we are inside the cliffs now.'

A minute passed without either of them speaking.

Drift pointed up ahead. 'Does that look like light to you?'

Felix squinted. She could see the faintest green glow. 'Come on, let's check it out.'

She walked faster, pulling Drift by the arm, and they soon found themselves in a much wider space. A green mist hung in the air, like they were in a witch's cauldron. Where was it coming from? Felix shivered.

Drift shone his torch upwards and it seemed like they were in a large dome-shaped space. 'Now this is what I call a creepy cave. If I was going to hide treasure, this would be the place.'

'Give me the torch. I'll have a look around and see what I can find,' said Felix.

'I'll come with you.'

'No, you wait here for Caspar.'

'Do I have to?'

'Yes.'

Felix followed the edge of the vast cave, wafting her hands to sweep the green mist away as she went. She couldn't help breathing it in as the mist surrounded her. A thick, musty taste filled her mouth.

Another blast of wind came from nowhere, swirling the mist around faster and faster, and pushing against Felix until she couldn't move her legs. She felt the torch being forced out of her hand. It smashed on the ground and the cave plunged into darkness.

'Felix! Help! Help me, please!' a faint voice called from the far end of the cave.

'Caspar? Drift, is Caspar with you?'

'Nope.'

'Help! Help me!'

'Caspar, where are you?' asked Felix, her eyes darting around.

She started to walk over to where the voice had come from, but something forming in the centre of the cave stopped her: amongst all the swirling mist a face appeared.

The face had rugged, creased skin and eyes that were so bloodshot they seemed to glow pure red. A long, greasy beard hung down from the face like seaweed.

It opened its ugly mouth in a twisted smile, revealing rotten teeth like gravestones.

A cold shiver ran all the way through Felix and she staggered backwards. She felt something sharp press against her back and turned to see a tall man standing behind her. His skin was the same colour as the sickly green mist that spun around him. In his hand he held a rusty sword, which he lifted up and pressed against Felix. She froze, not daring to move, her heart thumping.

Around the cave more men appeared out of the mist. To Felix's horror, they all looked in various stages of decay, their faces hollow and scarred, their clothes ragged. They had fierce expressions that made Felix's heart beat even faster. Were these the pirates of the *Tormenta*?

'Drift? Caspar?' she called.

She spotted Drift just to the left, squirming in the

grip of one of the men. There was no sign of Caspar.

A body appeared below the face in the centre of the cave, which made this man tower above all the others. His clothes were different to the other men's. He wore a long, blood-red cloak and a wide black hat over his matted hair.

There was something odd about him – about all the men, in fact. It was like they were only half there, like shadows or reflections, with a dull glow surrounding their bodies. Felix gasped as the realisation sunk in – these were ghosts.

The mist began to clear and the man in the cloak looked around at all the other men. Felix followed his gaze and finally saw Caspar over the other side of the cave, being held firmly. For a second she was relieved, but then she saw the sword held to his neck. He looked deathly pale.

'Get off him!' she called. 'Let go of Caspar!'

The man in the cloak seemed to float slowly towards her, his smile widening.

'Who … who are you?' she asked.

'I,' the man boomed, 'am Captain Traiton of the great ship *Tormenta*, and these are my men. But who, pray tell, are you?'

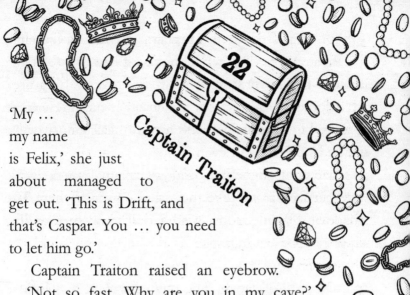

Captain Traiton

'My ...
my name
is Felix,' she just
about managed to
get out. 'This is Drift, and
that's Caspar. You ... you need
to let him go.'

Captain Traiton raised an eyebrow.
'Not so fast. Why are you in my cave?'

'We ... we were trying to find ... the treasure.'

'Oh, *my* treasure,' he said slowly. 'You mean that treasure over there?'

Captain Traiton pointed to the other end of the cave. Behind the circle of ghost pirates Felix could make out an alcove set back in the rock. At the end of this alcove was a large wooden chest.

Captain Traiton shrugged. 'Go ahead, take it.'

Felix frowned at him suspiciously. It couldn't be that easy, surely. But the pirates nearest to the chest shuffled out of the way, leaving a gap for her to get through, and the pirate's grip on her arm relaxed. Shaking slightly, she started to walk across the cave, feeling Captain Traiton's bloodshot eyes following her every move. She saw the treasure chest ahead of her, framed by rusty metal, with a golden lock on the front.

111

As she passed by the captain, she felt an icy chill run through her. This wasn't right – it had to be a trick. Instinct took over and she ran towards the treasure. At the same time, out of nowhere, a gigantic sword appeared in Captain Traiton's hand. It was almost twice the size of Felix and even in the dull light of the cave its sharp point shone menacingly. Captain Traiton might have been a ghost, but his sword was definitely real. He smiled and swung it towards her. Felix collapsed to the slippery floor just in time.

She heard Captain Traiton laughing, a cold, ear-splitting type of laugh. The pirates around him joined in, making the cave echo with evil cackling.

'You didn't think I would let you take it that easily, did you?'

'No,' Felix admitted, twisting round to look at him from the ground.

'And still you tried to get it.' Captain Traiton nodded approvingly. 'Braver than I thought, or maybe just stupid.' He rose up and glared down, his fiery eyes burning into her. 'A curse fated my men and me to be trapped on this earth as long as I claimed the treasure as my own. I have been in this cave for over two hundred and thirty long years. I am *not* going to give my treasure away to any soul that wanders in.'

'You were cursed?' asked Felix.

'Aye, we were. It was 1780 and I had just completed my greatest victory, capturing the *Tormenta* from its

Spanish crew…' And Captain Traiton told the story of the great battle … of meeting Esmeralda, the fortune-teller with the purple turban, locking her in the *Tormenta* and cutting her tongue out … how her prediction about the ship being wrecked had come true … and how the pirates had left her to drown in the shipwreck and taken their treasure into the cave.

So that's what happened the night Capston saw the Tormenta *sailing towards Thistlewick*, Felix realised.

It also explained the wailing. 'Esmeralda is still trapped in the shipwreck, as a ghost like you, isn't she?'

Maybe Esmeralda *had* been wailing to warn them against going into the cave.

'Aye, and she certainly likes to make a racket out there. That woman predicted the treasure's curse too,' Captain Traiton continued. 'We thought that it meant we would live for as long as we kept the treasure. Turns out that we died in this cave just like any man would. It's our ghosts that are trapped here with the treasure.'

'You must be sick of haunting this cave, then,' Drift spoke up. 'But we can help you. If you let us take the treasure, then your curse will be over. You won't be trapped here any more.'

Captain Traiton didn't move from above Felix, but turned to face Drift. 'Oh, I don't know. Let me think about that… How about, NO!'

Gritting her teeth, Felix thought hard, trying to come up with a way of getting out of this.

'A relative of yours, Tristan Traiton, is coming to find the treasure too,' said Drift.

'Yeah,' said Felix, trying to help Drift talk their way out of this. 'Tristan Traiton will be in Shark Fin Cove any minute.'

'Oh will he now? I imagine that must be my great-great-great-great-grandson.'

Felix nodded. 'You'd like him. He's an escaped criminal who stole loads of money.'

'If you let us go and get him, we can bring him here to collect the treasure and it will still be kept in your family,' said Drift.

'My family, ay? Well, after two hundred and thirty years together, it's these men here I think of as my family. If this Tristan Traiton wants my treasure he can come to this cave and settle it the old pirate way: by fighting me for it himself! But for now he isn't here and you are. I can see by the fear in your eyes that you are regretting entering my cave. You would like a way out of this mess you have got yourselves into, would you not?'

'Yes … please,' said Felix. She stood back up, her hopes rising a little.

'Very well. I can be kind,' he said with a wink to his men. 'These pirates have had hundreds of years without much in the way of entertainment. You can entertain them, Felix.'

'How?' she asked with a sinking feeling.

'By fighting me for the treasure!'

A cheer rang around the cave as the pirates waved their swords in the air.

'But we're only kids!' called Drift.

'Oh, *really*? I hadn't noticed,' Captain Traiton said sarcastically. 'You see young Tommo over there, one of my powder monkeys?'

He pointed and Felix turned to look at a small pirate on her right, wearing a bandanna. She guessed the ghost boy was about the same age as her.

'Tommo,' the captain asked, 'how many times did I threaten to beat you when you were alive?'

''undred's, Captain,' Tommo said in a thick accent.

'And how many times did I actually beat you?'

Tommo grinned. ''undreds, Captain. Beat me 'alf to death, you did!'

Captain Traiton turned back to Felix. 'You see, child or not, it makes no difference to me. So as I see it, there are three possible outcomes to your situation. There is only one way you can break the curse and get your hands on my treasure: you fight me for it, sword against sword, and you win.'

His men laughed at the idea that this would ever be a possibility.

'However, if you fight me and lose, all three of you will be doomed to stay here with us pirates forevermore, just like the last person who tried to take my treasure.'

'Someone else tried to take your treasure?' asked Felix.

'Aye, seventy-five years ago it must be now. A man named Barney. There he is, over there, holding onto your little friend.'

Felix noticed now that the ghost who held a sword to Caspar's throat was dressed differently to the rest of them. Rather than the filthy rags that the others were wearing, he had on a thick coat and cap a bit like Albert wore. His face, though, carried the same evil expression as the other men's as he stared straight at Felix.

'It took us every one of those years to convert Barney to our pirate ways. But now he is one of us, so don't think you'll get any help from him,' Captain Traiton explained.

'You said there were three outcomes,' said Felix. 'What's the third one?'

'Oh yes, I nearly forgot. Well, the two of you can, if you wish, run away now and we will do you no harm.'

'Two? But there are three of us.'

Captain Traiton chuckled to himself. 'As I said, you and that boy over there – Drift, isn't it? – you can run away. But if you do, we keep the other boy as our prize!'

'No, you can't do that!' shouted Felix.

Captain Traiton grinned at her – this was all a game to him.

'Well then,' he replied, 'make your choice.'

'Felix,' a quiet, shaking voice said. She turned to face Caspar as he spoke. 'You need to take the third option.'

'No, Caspar, we can't leave you here!'

'Just listen to me,' he replied. 'If you fight Captain

Traiton, then you will lose and we'll all be trapped here. But if you and Drift run away, then only I get trapped and you two survive. It makes sense. It's the best option we've got.'

Felix was aware that all the pirates were looking from her to Caspar and back again. It was sickening – this was *fun* for them.

'No, it doesn't make sense,' she argued. 'We've come all this way to get the treasure so that you can stay on Thistlewick. We're not leaving you here!'

'Felix, I'm not cut out to be an adventurer like you. I've held us up all the way along. Just leave me and run.'

Felix glared across at Drift. 'You heard Drift talking, didn't you?'

Caspar hung his head low.

'I didn't mean what I said,' said Drift from the opposite side of the cave. 'I don't think you're pathetic, Caspar. Saying what you just have and telling Felix and me to leave you here – that makes you braver than I could ever be.'

Caspar raised his eyes slightly and almost smiled.

'Well I hate to break up this *lovely* chat of yours,' said Captain Traiton, 'but I must ask you to make your decision.'

Felix blocked out all her fear and stared straight at the pirate captain as fiercely as she could. 'Caspar forgot one thing.'

'Oh, and what's that?'

'That none of us are going to get trapped here. I will fight you, Captain Traiton, and I will win that treasure!' Determination buzzed through her. She wasn't going to give up.

'Very well,' Captain Traiton replied, smiling to reveal his rotten teeth again. 'Oh, and one more thing: when we fight, under pirate law, we fight to the death!'

The Fight

'Give the girl your sword, Skinner,' Captain Traiton ordered.

'Aye, Captain.'

Skinner pulled his weapon from his belt and thrust it into her hand. Compared to Captain Traiton's sword this one was small and rusty, but it was far heavier than she expected and she had to grip it firmly to avoid dropping it.

'Another pirate law. You require someone to second you. A person who will take your place if you should fail. My second is Skinner. Which of your friends is yours?'

'I'll do it. I'll be Felix's second,' said Drift.

'Very well, then we are ready. Skinner, you can start proceedings.'

Felix's whole body was tense with fear as Skinner pushed her forwards towards Captain Traiton. The other ghosts moved in to form a tight circle around them, hustling with each other to get the best position to view the fight.

'Gentlemen,' Skinner began, and many of the pirates chuckled. 'Or rather, Captain and ... girl. You will fight each other with swords. The victor will be the man ... or girl ... who kills the other, and they shall win all the treasure in this cave. I will say "one, two, three, attack". At the last word, you can attack at will. Are you ready?'

Felix gritted her teeth. 'Yes.'

'Yes,' Captain Traiton hissed.

'One,' said Skinner.

Felix couldn't help thinking what a hopeless situation this was. She'd had sword fights with Drift before, but they were only pretend, using wooden sticks to poke each other. Drift always beat her. It was one of the few things he was better at than her.

'Two.'

So how was she supposed to fight a pirate captain holding a real sword twice the size of hers? And this was a fight to the death. *She* could die easily enough, but how on earth was she meant to kill a ghost?

'Three.'

She looked at Captain Traiton. He was staring around at his pirates, who were all cheering for him, firing him up like fans at a boxing match. All Felix could think might work was to take him by surprise.

'Attack!'

As soon as Skinner said this, Felix shot towards Captain Traiton like a bullet. She swung her sword at him. He barely moved his, and the two swords connected with a clang of metal on metal. Felix's sword bounced off Captain Traiton's and she stumbled to the ground on her knees.

Captain Traiton leered down at her and she held her sword up in a feeble defence. Panic started to build up inside her and she struggled to breathe through it. The captain lifted his giant sword up and smashed it down powerfully on hers, cutting it clean in half, the two broken parts of the sword clattering to the ground next to her.

Horrified, she looked up at Captain Traiton. He raised his sword in the air and roared. 'YAAAAARRRRR!'

The pirates around him yelled back their support.

'Get her a new sword,' he bellowed. Immediately, another pirate floated forwards and dropped his sword next to Felix. 'Stand up, girl!'

'Go on, Felix,' she heard Drift call.

She saw Caspar firmly in Barney's grip behind Captain Traiton. Fear filled his eyes.

Captain Traiton puffed out his chest. 'Are you just going to stand there, or are you going to fight me?'

Without any other choice, Felix threw herself into it, swinging her sword left and right and left again. Captain Traiton casually knocked off all her blows. It was clear he was just having fun, like a cat playing with a mouse before eating it.

A chant of 'Captain! Captain! Captain!' came from the circle of pirates.

At this he directed his sword at Felix, and his facial expression changed from amusement to pure evil. His sword was so big that he had to hold it up high in order to swing it down at her. This gave Felix enough time to raise her sword up in defence. But when the swords hit, it sent a huge, painful shock through her body and she staggered to stay upright. Captain Traiton changed tactic and took a swipe at Felix's legs. She jumped up just in time to avoid the sharp point of his sword.

'Getting clever, are we?' he spat at her.

She raised her sword up to try another attack, but he quickly knocked the sword clean out of her hand and it flew to the hard ground. Felix scrambled towards it, grabbing hold of the hilt. But when she turned around, the end of Captain Traiton's sword was pointing at her face. She backed down and lay trembling against the floor. His sword followed her, millimetres away from touching.

'Which would you prefer to lose? Your nose, or your left eye?' he asked.

'Go for the nose!' a pirate called out.

'No, the eye!' said another.

'Nose!' called out a few more.

'Eye! Eye!'

'Noooose!'

Captain Traiton turned back to Felix, his eyes bulging in a bloodthirsty look. 'It's been decided. The nose it is!'

'YAAAAARRRRR!' cried the pirates.

Captain Traiton lowered his sword until Felix felt it on the tip of her nose. She closed her eyes tightly and waited for the worst to happen.

And waited.

Nothing. Then…

'Aarrg!' she heard Captain Traiton cry.

She opened her eyes just in time to see Drift jumping at the captain from behind. In the commotion he must have managed to get free and steal one of the pirates' swords. Before Captain Traiton had a chance to defend himself, Drift swung his sword and plunged it into the pirate captain's heart – or where his heart would be if he still had one. Captain Traiton jolted forwards, a puzzled frown creasing his face. He stood there, motionless, as Drift held the sword in his chest.

'You've done it, Drift! You've actually done it! You've defeated him!' Felix couldn't believe it.

But Captain Traiton's eyes brightened and his mouth cracked into a wide, mad grin.

'You forget,' he said, 'that this is a fight to the death.'

Felix watched in horror as the sword inside Captain Traiton started to glow bright red, as if it was heating up. Cracks appeared in it, quickly multiplying and combining. Drift let go of the sword with a cry of pain and it shattered to the floor in a thousand pieces. The pirates all laughed ferociously.

Felix felt sick. They had absolutely no chance if that's what happened to a sword inside a ghost.

'Get that boy away from me,' Captain Traiton ordered. 'Tie him up.'

As Drift was being dragged away, Felix heard a noise. It started faintly but grew and grew – it was the wailing of the fortune-teller from the sea. It was so deafening, she clutched her ears and rolled around on the floor in agony.

She could just about hear Captain Traiton yelling at her through the noise.

'Girl! Get up, girl! It won't be any fun if you don't fight back!'

'Can't you hear the wailing?' she cried out.

'Wailing? There's no wailing now. Stop fooling about and fight me!'

Why was she the only one who could hear Esmeralda?

The pirates' chants of 'Fight! Fight! Fight! Fight!' mixed with the wailing and made her head spin. She staggered up to the cheers and jeers of the pirates and stared at the blurred Captain Traiton in front of her.

She needed to concentrate, to focus, but she couldn't think. She screamed in desperation and it seemed to help, joining together with Esmeralda's wail to give her an extra boost of energy. She kept screaming and charged towards Captain Traiton.

To her surprise, the ghost captain only just managed to get his sword up in time to defend against Felix's quick movements. It looked like Drift must have slowed him down at least, and the captain's attacks weren't as frequent. She hoped if she could pierce Captain Traiton's ghost with *her* sword, that might slow him down even more.

He lunged at her and she staggered back a few paces. She focused on the wailing in her head and matched it with her own scream again, then took a running jump, flying up at Captain Traiton. She managed to get far higher in the air than she'd expected and swung her sword at his head. She saw the pure rage in his eyes as she got closer – now centimetres away from hitting her target. A roar came out of his mouth then, almost louder than the wailing in her head. It sent a torrent of air shooting at her with such force that she was blown back over the circle of ghost pirates.

Felix felt herself slam against the wall of the cave with a sickening thud and she collapsed in a heap on the ground.

For a few seconds there was nothing – just blackness and silence. Then Felix regained consciousness.

All she could hear now was the wailing. She opened one eye a slit and saw a pirate glancing down at her. He turned back to Captain Traiton and ran a finger across his neck. The pirate crew waved their arms and swords – they must think she was dead. Captain Traiton put a finger to his mouth and pointed to Drift. Skinner untied him and gave him a sword. Drift briefly looked over at Felix, his face full of shock, then charged at Captain Traiton.

From her position, Felix could only half see the fight. Captain Traiton was even slower now he had used so much energy roaring at her, and Drift was swinging his sword at every part of his ghostly form. But even with the pirate captain at half-strength, he was too powerful. Drift kept getting knocked down, jumping straight back up, only to be knocked down again.

Felix closed her eyes. She let the wailing in her head take over. She thought of poor Esmeralda, trapped and drowned on the ship. The fortune-teller had probably been wailing to warn them not to go into the cave earlier, but Felix hadn't listened.

Amongst the wailing, Felix suddenly heard something else. It was a voice – trying to say something.

'FEEEELIIIIX!'

I can hear you, Esmeralda, she thought, concentrating even harder on the fortune-teller.

The wailing changed. It was still a horrible cry, but it had a different pitch.

'WHHHY … WHHHY?'

Why what, Esmeralda?

'THE TREASUUURE! WHHHY?'

It took Felix a second to realise what she meant.

Why do we want the treasure? Because we need it to help my friend Caspar stay on Thistlewick. But it's no good! We'll never get it.

She let the fortune-teller's wail flood over her again.

You sound in so much pain, Esmeralda. If we could beat

Captain Traiton and break the curse, that would free you, wouldn't it? You wouldn't be trapped any more. I wish we could help you. But I'm sorry. He's too strong. There's no way we can beat him.

Through the wailing, the voice came again. 'BREEAAAK! BREEAAAK!'

Break what, Esmeralda? Break what?

'BREEAAAK THE CHESSST ... TO BREEAAAK ... THE CUUURSE!'

Break the chest to break the curse? Felix questioned.

'BREEAAAK THE CHESSST TO BREEAAAK THE CUUURSE!' came the words again.

Then all was silent. No more wailing.

Felix opened her eyes, her heart pounding.

'Thank you, Esmeralda,' she mouthed.

So Captain Traiton was wrong! They didn't have to beat him in a fight to break the curse and get his treasure. They had to break into his treasure chest!

She stared hard, through all the ghosts and the fighting, and could just make out the chest over on the other side of the cave. There was no way she would be able to get there without being noticed. Caspar was much closer to the treasure, but he was in the firm grip of Barney.

Captain Traiton's sword smashed down onto Drift's, sending him flying to the ground. The captain bent down over him.

'Now, let me see. What will it be for the boy? Left hand, or right foot? What do you think, men?'

Felix stood up. She could just about see the treasure chest over the top of the jeering pirates and the bent figure of Captain Traiton. Her aim would have to be perfect, but she had no other choice – not if she was to save Drift and get the treasure.

She grabbed hold of her sword and held it like a javelin. Using her other arm to point at the treasure chest she took aim, throwing the sword high in the air with all her strength. The pirates were fixed on Captain Traiton and Drift and none of them seemed to notice as the sword glided quickly over the top of them and headed straight for the chest. Felix held her breath.

At that moment Captain Traiton called out, 'The left hand it is! And no one's going to save *you*, boy.'

'Please, no!' cried Drift.

Captain Traiton stood up tall and held his sword high, ready to strike.

'No!' called Felix. She watched, as if in slow motion, as the sword she had thrown travelled all the way through the captain's ghostly body, which was now right in its path. It clattered to the ground behind him.

'Felix!' called Drift.

Captain Traiton turned to glare at her. 'I thought you were dead!'

He shot towards Felix, his sword aimed straight at her head. She looked past him. Her sword sat there on the ground, glowing red and starting to crack – and just a metre away from Caspar.

'Caspar! Grab the sword. Quick, before it breaks up! Grab it and stab the chest!' Felix shouted.

Caspar struggled, but Barney had too strong a hold on him. They'd lost. Felix really was going to die now.

But then she saw Barney look at Caspar. Caspar whispered something in his ear. At this, Barney turned to face Felix and no longer had the menacing stare of the evil man Captain Traiton had turned him into. His eyes were peaceful and as he smiled at her, he loosened his grip on Caspar.

What had Caspar said to change Barney like this?

Felix didn't have time to think about it. Cries rang up from the other pirates and Captain Traiton turned away from Felix just in time to see Caspar running for the sword.

'The boy!' the captain yelled. 'Get him!'

Although it was glowing a fiery red, Caspar grabbed hold of the sword and turned around. At least ten pirates started to pile down on him. Barney grabbed hold of them, trying to clear them out of Caspar's way, but it was no good – yet more ghosts shot towards him. Felix could only watch from the other side of the cave as Caspar closed his eyes and charged into all the ghosts, the sword stretched out in front of him. Somehow he got through them and Felix's hopes rose, but after the sword's impact with so many ghosts it was now white with heat and sparks flew from it. Caspar yelled out but still he kept going.

He was metres away from the treasure chest, but Felix knew the sword was seconds away from shattering into a thousand pieces. With one last effort Caspar dived for the chest.

The end of the white-hot sword plunged into the wood.

The pirates around Caspar froze. For a few seconds no one moved.

Then the sword, glowing as bright as a star, exploded. Sparks of fire shot out like a thousand fireworks, setting the chest on fire. Blazing wood flew in every direction and the floor of the cave was strewn with the burning remains of the treasure chest.

Captain Traiton watched this happen, then turned back to Felix. The last thing she remembered was the stone-cold stare from his blood-red eyes as he swung his sword straight at her. 'YAAAAARRRRR!'

And then, nothing.

All was dark.

Treasure!

'Felix! Felix!'

She felt some-one shaking her and slowly opened her eyes. Drift was staring down at her.

'Captain Traiton!' Felix looked over Drift's shoulder, but saw no one. 'Where is he? And the other pirates?'

'Gone, Felix. They disappeared when the treasure chest broke.'

'Wow! It worked. Where ... where's Caspar?' she asked, remembering what he had done, and how brave he had been.

'He's over there, by the treasure.' Drift pointed. 'And Felix, there's loads of it!'

Drift helped her to her feet and they walked across the cave. Apart from the various swords scattered on the ground, there was no sign that a large group of pirates had ever been here. The green mist had cleared and the air now had a golden shine to it, which came from where Caspar was kneeling, examining a piece of broken wood.

'Thank you, Caspar. You saved us! Thank you!'

She ran up and gave him a hug. She noticed the hand that he'd held the sword in.

'Caspar, your hand, it's burnt! Are you OK?'

He smiled at her. 'I'm fine, Felix. Look! Look at all the treasure.'

Felix turned now and saw it. Scattered all over the rocky surface was a huge collection of gold coins, gems of every colour, crowns and other things that Felix didn't recognise, but that looked like they were made out of silver.

'Wooooow!'

'We did it, Felix, we actually did it!' said Caspar, his eyes wide.

'But, Caspar, what did you say to Barney? Why did he let you go?'

'While you were fighting, I asked him why he had tried to find the treasure seventy-five years ago. He told me he had been caring for his baby granddaughter, who was really ill, and he'd needed lots of money to pay for her medicine. He's been angry with himself ever since he was killed, thinking his granddaughter must have died because he had abandoned her and failed to get the treasure. But I was able to tell him that she is still alive.'

'How do you know that?' asked Drift.

'Because his full name is Barney Didsbury. Mrs Didsbury is his granddaughter! He was so pleased to know she didn't die, and that she's still alive. Then when you threw the sword, Felix, Barney asked me what we wanted the treasure for. When I told him, he just said "run" and let me go.'

Felix smiled and said to the air, 'Thank you, Barney.'

They began gathering up as much of the treasure as they could, but they only had Drift's rucksack and their schoolbags to carry it. Still, they filled these to the brim with the larger pieces of treasure. Then they stuffed their pockets full of gold coins and gems.

Felix looked back at the pile of sparkling treasure still on the ground – there was so much left. 'We'll have to come back for the rest.'

They headed back through the cave. Near the entrance, Felix saw Captain Traiton's gigantic sword lying on the ground. She tried lifting it up but it was far too heavy. She was determined to take it – they'd have to find a way of carrying it when they came back to get the rest of the treasure.

Although Felix was weighed down by all the treasure, the journey back along the tunnel seemed to take no time at all, and they were soon out in the bright afternoon sunshine of Shark Fin Cove. There was no wailing coming from the sea now.

'So how are we going to get out of here?' asked Drift.

'The only way out of Shark Fin Cove is back up the cliff,' said Felix. 'It'll take us a few climbs to get all the treasure up there.'

'Then what are we waiting for?' asked Caspar. 'Let's start climbing.'

Drift grinned at him. 'You've changed.'

He nudged Felix, but something had caught her eye – a small ripple in the sea. She walked up to the edge of the water, watching the ripple grow bigger until something rose up out of it. With the sun shining in her eyes it was hard to see what it was. She squinted and could just make out what looked like the figure of a pale woman wearing a purple turban, floating above the water.

'Thank you for your help, Esmeralda,' she whispered.

'*And thank you, Felix,*' she heard in her mind, and this time the voice was gentle and clear. '*You have freed me. You deserve the treasure.*'

Felix turned to Caspar and Drift to see if they had noticed Esmeralda – but they were looking the other way, their eyes wide.

Felix turned to follow their gaze. A small boat had appeared at the other end of the cove, and out of it stepped Tristan Traiton.

'Well, well, well,' he said, his voice as dark as his greasy black hair. 'I see you have done all the work for me, children. This makes my life very easy indeed.'

'*Another Traiton?*' Esmeralda asked.

'How did you know that?' asked Felix.

'*I can feel the same evil presence coming from him that I felt in Captain Traiton.*'

Felix watched Tristan Traiton stride up the beach towards Drift and Caspar.

'You will take that treasure over to my boat.' He pulled a small black gun out of his back pocket and pointed it at them. 'Or else!'

Drift took a step back, Caspar took three. They looked at each other, not knowing what to do. But Felix smiled. After fighting and defeating a whole crew of ghost pirates, she was no longer scared of her fake head teacher, not even with a gun.

She turned back to Esmeralda. 'I don't suppose you'd be able to help again, would you?'

Esmeralda looked at Felix, a twinkle in her eyes. *'Two Traitons in one day? It would be my pleasure.'*

The fortune-teller raised her thin arms and pointed them towards the boat Tristan Traiton had used to get here. Out of the boat, a length of rope appeared, rising up in the air. Felix gasped as it shot towards Tristan Traiton, like a snake pouncing on a mouse.

'Aaaaarrrggg!' he cried as the rope grabbed hold of his gun and whipped it out of his hand.

The gun flew high into the air and came to land in the water near Felix, where it promptly sank.

The rope coiled around Tristan Traiton's shoulders, pulling him backwards and flinging him into the boat, where it wrapped around his whole body. He started yelling out. A piece of the boat's sail ripped itself off and wrapped around his mouth, forcing him into silence. Felix watched with delight as he squirmed and tried to get the rope off, but he was held much too tightly.

'Thank you, again, Esmeralda,' said Felix.

Esmeralda smiled. '*Now, I am free, so it is my time to go. Goodbye, Felix.*'

The ghost of the fortune-teller rose up into the blue sky. Felix didn't take her eyes off her until the image of Esmeralda merged with the golden sun and she was gone.

'Who was *that*?' asked Drift, coming alongside Felix.

'She was … a very special person,' Felix settled on saying. 'Now, do you think you could sail us back home in that?' She pointed at the boat, where Tristan Traiton had given up his struggle and simply stared out furiously.

'Of course,' replied Drift.

'Well, then, let's fill it up with treasure.'

***

It took three more trips into the cave to bring out all the treasure, and a further trip just to carry out Captain Traiton's sword, which they managed between the three of them.

They jumped into the boat, sitting amongst the treasure, and Drift fired up the boat's engine. Soon Felix felt the wind rushing through her hair as they cut through the waves.

The sight of Tristan Traiton lying at the back of the boat surrounded by so much treasure that he couldn't touch was brilliant. His face had turned bright red with anger and Felix thought he might explode.

'I don't think we should let anyone know we've got all this treasure. Not yet, anyway,' said Felix. 'We need to think about how we can use it to keep you and your mum on Thistlewick, Caspar.'

Caspar nodded.

'I think I know the perfect hiding place for it,' said Drift. He stared at Tristan Traiton. 'But we don't want *him* knowing where it is.'

Felix found another piece of cloth in the boat and used it to blindfold the fake head teacher.

It seemed to take only ten minutes from leaving Shark Fin Cove to Drift mooring the boat up in a cove just along from the harbour in the south of Thistlewick. He pointed over to a small cave carved into the rocks.

'Your secret hideout,' Felix realised. 'Good idea.'

Having just found the treasure in a cave, it felt really weird hiding it away again, but at least they knew that when they came to fetch it, there would be no evil surprises waiting for them.

'Now,' said Felix, once all the treasure was out of the boat, 'shall we take our prisoner round to the harbour to see your dad, Drift?'

***

They spotted Drift's dad busy in conversation with a

very tall policewoman and a very round policeman as they reached the harbour.

'So there's no sign of them?' he asked, not yet noticing their arrival.

'We carried out a full search of the Forest of Shadows and there were no children in there,' said the tall policewoman. 'We did find this dog wandering around, though. He looked very lost.'

Felix noticed a large dog with a shaggy mane of chocolate-brown fur, on a lead at the round policeman's side.

'That's Farmer Potts's dog, Sparky,' said Drift's dad. 'He's been missing for a week.'

Felix stood up in the boat then, and Sparky spotted her. He pulled away from the round policeman and ran over to the jetty next to the boat. He jumped up at her, wagging his tail, and Felix laughed as she realised something.

'We've met Sparky before, Caspar.'

Caspar stroked the dog's head. 'Have we? Where?'

'In the forest! I think this is the *wolf* we were so scared of.'

'But … he looks nothing like a wolf.'

'It must have been his shadow that made him look so scary. The Forest of Shadows was playing tricks on us.' Felix looked up then, realising that three pairs of eyes were staring at her – the two police officers' and Drift's dad's.

'Drift, are you in that boat too?' he asked sternly.

'Hi, Dad,' said Drift, standing up next to Felix and Caspar.

The fisherman strode over to the jetty. 'Where on earth have you been? And what are you doing in the boat I hired out to Mr Foxsworth? You are meant to be at home, Drift. Felix and Caspar, your mums are worried sick. They say you've been missing since yesterday. These police officers have been looking all over the island for you. Explain yourselves!'

'Sorry, Mr Castle, but there's a good reason – we've captured a dangerous criminal,' said Felix.

'You've what?' asked the tall policewoman.

Felix, Drift and Caspar stepped out of the way to reveal Tristan Traiton at the back of the boat. He was squirming in his cocoon of ropes again.

'What have you done to Mr Foxsworth?!' asked Drift's dad, looking at the three children with a deep frown.

'Mr Foxsworth isn't his real name. This is Tristan Traiton,' Caspar explained. 'He escaped from an English prison last month.'

Tristan Traiton started making strange groaning sounds. The round policeman stepped over to the boat and untied the pieces of cloth that covered his eyes and mouth.

Taking a deep breath, Tristan Traiton spoke in a panting, high-pitched voice. 'Please, get me out of this rope. Don't believe anything these children say. They are lying about me.'

The police officers stared at each other and Drift's dad glared at his son. Felix could tell they weren't sure who to believe.

Then she remembered something Caspar had said when they had found the newspaper articles in his office.

She stepped over to Tristan Traiton and grabbed hold of his thick black hair.

'Don't you dare,' he growled.

She pulled and the hair came clean away from his head.

Everyone gasped.

'You were right, Caspar, it was a wig!'

There, on the back of Tristan Traiton's neck, was the giant tattooed letter T.

'See, we're telling the truth!' said Drift. 'He's only been pretending to be a head teacher, Dad.'

'If you don't believe us, you can find some newspaper articles hidden behind a map in his office,' said Caspar.

The police officers looked at each other.

'What do you think, Inspector Cooper?' the round policeman asked the tall policewoman.

'Well, PC Dan, it looks to me like the children are right. In fact, I recognise that tattoo on the back of his neck from the police database. This man is right at the top of our most wanted list. We came here to find missing children, and we'll leave with an escaped criminal. I'd say that's a good day's work,' said the tall policewoman. 'Let's get him out of the boat.'

Felix watched with a big grin on her face as they went over and lifted the fake head teacher out of the boat.

'Tristan Traiton, I am arresting you for—'

'They're lying, I tell you, lying!' the fake head teacher shouted out.

He tried to put up a fight, but there wasn't much he could do with rope wrapped round him.

'I've been framed! Set up!'

The police officers started to drag him away, and with both legs tied together, he had to hop to keep up.

'Goodbye, *Traitor Traiton*!' Felix said triumphantly, then burst out laughing. Drift and Caspar quickly joined in.

Tristan Traiton looked back at them and let out an angry scream. His eyes widened and Felix, Drift and Caspar continued to laugh as his face grew redder and redder.

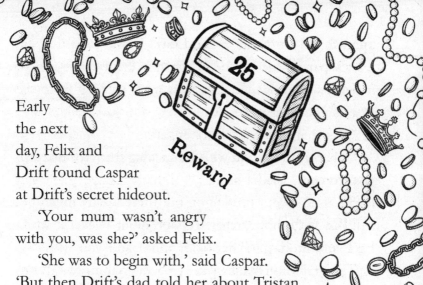

Early
the next
day, Felix and
Drift found Caspar
at Drift's secret hideout.

'Your mum wasn't angry
with you, was she?' asked Felix.

'She was to begin with,' said Caspar.
'But then Drift's dad told her about Tristan
Traiton and she got really angry about the fact
our head teacher wasn't really a head teacher. Then
she decided she was actually really proud of me for
finding out the truth about him.'

'I really thought I was going to get grounded, but my
mum reacted like yours,' said Felix.

'What are you holding there, Caspar?' asked Drift.

Caspar showed them a piece of wood. 'I found
this with the treasure yesterday. I think it's part of the
treasure chest.'

Caspar showed the wood to Felix. There was writing
on it in faint gold letters:

Propiedad del gobierno español 1780⁴

'Is that Spanish? What does it mean?' she asked.

'I looked it up on the computer,' said Caspar. 'It
translates as "property of the Spanish government".'

'So Captain Traiton stole the treasure from the

Spanish government?' asked Drift.

Caspar nodded. 'And if Tristan Traiton had got to it before us, he would also have been stealing from the Spanish government.'

'But that means…' Felix began.

'That if we keep it, we'll be stealing from the Spanish government,' said Caspar. 'I think we have to give it back.'

'But we can't do that. If we give it back we won't have any money to give your mum and you won't be able to stay on Thistlewick. After everything we did to get that treasure, we…' Felix paused as she noticed the expression on Caspar's face – he didn't look upset. 'Hang on, is there something you're not telling us?'

'Look at the numbers next to the writing.' Caspar pointed to them.

'What about them?'

'The Spanish government used to use different codes to identify all their treasure. I typed that code into a Spanish government website. It turns out they're still looking for this treasure.'

'OK,' said Felix slowly.

'And there's a reward for anyone who finds it.'

'How much?' asked Drift.

'Twenty-two thousand euros,' said Caspar, now with a big smile on his face.

'Is that enough for your mum, so you can stay here?' asked Felix.

Caspar's grin widened even further. 'Definitely.'

A rush of excitement ran through Felix. She leapt forwards and hugged him. 'What are we waiting for? Let's give this treasure back to the Spanish government!' She paused. 'Wait – how exactly do we do that?'

'I think we're going to need Mayor Merryweather's help,' said Caspar.

'But won't we have to tell him how we found the treasure?' asked Drift.

Felix looked at Caspar uncertainly.

'I think,' he said thoughtfully, 'that my mum would never let me out of the house again if she found out what really happened at Shark Fin Cove.'

Felix nodded. 'My mum too. We've got to keep it a secret.'

'You're right,' Drift agreed. 'But where are we going to say the treasure came from?'

Felix had an idea. 'We can tell Mayor Merryweather we found it in Tristan Traiton's boat and that he was trying to steal it.'

'Great thinking! And that's partly true, anyway,' said Drift.

'Right.' Felix looked from Drift to Caspar and they shared a grin. 'Let's go and see Mayor Merryweather.'

***

Felix felt the blood rushing to her head.

She was determined to do a longer handstand than Drift, even if it gave her a headache.

'Ten more seconds and you'll have beaten him,' said Caspar, who was timing her.

It had been a busy couple of weeks. Mayor Merryweather had been on the phone to various important people in the Spanish government and they had been to collect the treasure, leaving behind a cheque for twenty-two thousand euros made out to Amber Littlepage, Caspar's mum. She burst into tears when Felix, Caspar and Drift gave it to her.

Tristan Traiton had been re-arrested and was waiting to be sent back to prison in England for a very long time. It turned out there was also a big reward for finding this escaped criminal, and they all agreed the second reward should also go to Caspar's mum. Together with the money from the Spanish government, it meant that Mrs Littlepage didn't have to rent a house on Thistlewick any more. She had enough money for a deposit to buy one – Caspar would be staying on Thistlewick for good!

'Five seconds, Felix!' Caspar said now. He hadn't stopped smiling all week.

Felix's hands started to wobble but she just managed to hold on.

'You've done it!' shouted Caspar.

'Yes! I'm the handstand champion!' Felix collapsed to the floor. 'I win the bet and you owe me a gold coin,' she said to Drift.

'But it's my last one.' Drift took the piece of treasure out of his pocket.

'And I won it fair and square.'

Caspar looked from Felix to Drift with a frown. 'I thought we'd given all the treasure back to the Spanish government?'

'Well,' said Felix, grinning, 'not *all* the treasure. We accidentally forgot about a few pieces we'd put in our pockets. Anyway, I'm sure the Spanish government won't mind after all the effort we put into finding the treasure.' She pulled a small bag out of her pocket and showed Caspar three gold coins and a couple of gems. 'Here, you can have a gold coin and a gem.'

She tossed them to him and Caspar caught them neatly, smiling. They set off along the coastal path, heading home.

'I'm going to win that coin back off you, you know,' Drift said to Felix.

'How?' she asked.

Drift thought for a second. 'I bet you, for that gold coin, that I can hold my breath for longer than you.'

'Too easy!' said Felix. 'I bet you I can last for longer than you without having a wash.'

'No, I bet you—'

'I bet,' Caspar interrupted Drift, 'that you two can't go a whole day without having a bet.'

Felix and Drift looked at each other.

'Spoilsport,' said Drift, but then he winked at Caspar.

Felix put her arm around her best friend. 'What would we do without you, Caspar?'

'Get into a lot more trouble, probably,' Caspar said with a straight face. They all burst out laughing.

***

Later that night, Felix lay in bed, but she couldn't get to sleep. Everything that had happened was running around her head.

Well, Felix, she told herself, *you've defeated a ghost pirate, discovered an escaped criminal, but most importantly, you've stopped Caspar from having to leave Thistlewick. That's better than all the treasure in the world!*

She grinned and stared up at her bedroom wall. Hung there, almost as long as the wall itself, was Captain Traiton's sword, its silver edge shining brightly in the light of the full moon.

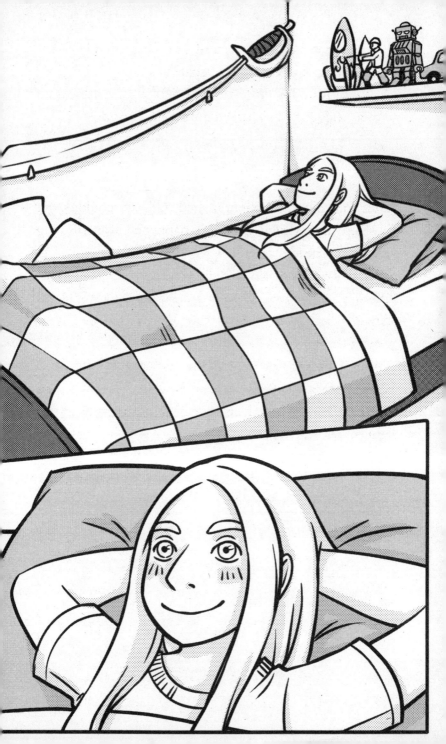

Felix's adventures continue in book 2!

50 years ago:
Amelie is trapped in her bedroom in Murkhill Mansion, with only her diary and her rag toys to keep her company.

Today: When exploring the abandoned Murkhill Mansion, Felix, Caspar and Drift find Amelie's diary. Strange things start to happen – the rooms mix themselves up in an impossible maze and the mansion turns into a nightmare world that the children cannot escape from. Then Drift goes missing.

Everything that is happening seems to be connected to Amelie and her diary. But what is turning her nightmares into reality? Can Felix and Caspar find Drift? And what will happen when Amelie's rag toys mutate into something far creepier and more dangerous?

FELIX DASHWOOD AND THE
TRAITOR'S REVENGE

LUKE TEMPLE

... and in book 3!

Caspar is acting strangely and it has something to do with a mysterious ship that has appeared off the coast of Thistlewick Island. Felix and Drift sneak onto the ship to investigate. There, they encounter a dark, creepy woman with a crystal ball, and realise that she is hypnotising Caspar in order to find out information. But the woman isn't in charge of the ship – she is working for someone else. A man who wants revenge on Felix and will destroy the whole of Thistlewick to get it.

Felix is captured by a ghostly white mist, which ties her up like rope. Unable to escape, she looks up at the giant, shadowy figure that appears above her ... at his menacing, bloodshot eyes. Who is it that is taking his revenge on her?

www.luketemple.co.uk

Luke Temple's 'Ghost Island' series:

When the world-famous ghost hunter, Spooky Steve, investigates Becky's home above the post office, the ghost of Walter Anion appears and curses the place. Can Becky figure out how to stop this curse, before everything she knows and loves is destroyed forever?

Becky and Finn get trapped inside the abandoned Thicket House by a monsterous ghost, known as 'the spectre'. As the spectre's evil plans become clear, they have to battle their fears and fight for their lives. Can they escape from Thicket House before it's too late?

www.luketemple.co.uk